S0-BYA-965

"YOU'RE OFF THE CASE, McQ!"

Chief Grogan said it, but obviously all the top brass gathered in this room had decided. They were convinced they had a radical plot on their hands. They didn't want McQ, who had a reputation for the brand of persuasion defense lawyers called brutality. This was a case for a man with public relations sense.

McQ protested, his voice cool but urgent, "Santiago is the biggest dealer in the city. His inflow's under pressure now. Stan could have tipped to something. They'd have to bump him if he knew something . . ."

"That's it," Grogan interrupted. "Until further notice you're at a desk."

Quietly, methodically, McQ shed his tools. He put his I.D. card down on the table, then his handcuffs, his service revolver.

IF THEY WOULDN'T LET HIM CHASE DOWN STAN BOYLE'S KILLER AS A COP —HE'D DO IT ON HIS OWN!

Books By Alexander Edwards

McQ
The Last of Sheila

Published By
WARNER PAPERBACK LIBRARY

McQ

A Novel by
Alexander Edwards
Based on a Screenplay by
Lawrence Roman

**WARNER
PAPERBACK
LIBRARY**

A Warner Communications Company

WARNER PAPERBACK LIBRARY EDITION
FIRST PRINTING: FEBRUARY, 1974

WARNER PAPERBACK LIBRARY IS A DIVISION OF WARNER BOOKS, INC.
75 ROCKEFELLER PLAZA, NEW YORK, N.Y. 10019.

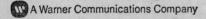 A Warner Communications Company

McQ

CHAPTER I

This was the part of the job he liked best. When the outcome was sure, final. When he was in control of when, where and how. He was a purposeful man, methodical and unhurried. Not for him the wheelings and the dealings, the secret phone calls in the night, the talk of big money and involved transactions. He was a man of action, with little patience for indecision and even less for bullshit.

He kept his mind empty as he slipped the rubber surgical gloves slowly and carefully onto his large, hairy hands, smoothing the thin latex over each finger, then flexing and unflexing his hands to make certain the fit was perfect. Designed for the operating room, the gloves insured complete coverage with perfect mobility; they were ideal for the job at hand. Now, slowly and with equal patience, the big man unfolded a pair of new stretch rubbers, the kind that fitted into their own plastic pack for tucking into attaché cases. Matching heel to heel and toe to toe with precision, he bent to fit the rubbers over his shoes, tugging at them slightly to adjust them to precise perfection. One over the left shoe; one over the right. It wasn't raining. He stamped his feet lightly to check the fit, and smiled in satisfaction. Then he let himself think about the job at hand, and the smile grew broader. This was the part he would like best.

In no way hampered by the surgical gloves, the big man took up the zippered leather case on the seat beside him, briefly and unconsciously fondling the leather before tugging at the zipper tab. Inside the case a clear plastic bag was wrapped lovingly and protectively around a .38. Its six-inch barrel gleamed even through the plastic film; it was an obviously well-cared-for weapon. The man's expression softened, as at the sight of an old friend, but the dark glasses he wore masked the softening, leaving only a touch of it around the rugged lines of the controlled mouth. Removing the gun from its plastic wrapper, he checked the chambers; four bullets, that should be plenty. He replaced the gun neatly in the plastic bag and laid it gently back in its zippered case, which he tucked securely next to him on the seat. Then he turned the key in the ignition and stepped on the gas pedal.

The '72 Chevy cruised slowly in the darkness. Around it the streets of the city flowed and changed from industrial to commercial to residential. A large city, vital, heterogenous, Seattle had it all. High rises and low slums, black ghettos and mansions on the green, the blue waters of Puget Sound and the mountains with caps of ice, Rainier looking like a Japanese woodblock. The car's headlights pierced the darkness, the savage eyes of some great nocturnal animal tracking its prey, and behind the dark glasses the tall man's eyes scanned the night streets with the patience of a hunter, looking, looking.

Officer Hyatt rattled the gate of the hardware store, checking to see that it was securely locked. Satisfied, he plodded slowly and quietly to the next store on the dark, silent block. It was a neighborhood of small stores and two-story houses that held, for the most part, elderly tenants long past ambition or dreams. The padlocks and gates on their little businesses were like the shutterings of their own lives, and Hyatt's too. The man fit the beat; his growing belly poked through his uniform shirt, his shoulders sagged with the long, weary miles of walking and checking, back and forth. A dependable police officer without imagination or spectacular bravery, Hyatt was a cop close to retirement and glad of it. This small section of securely locked doors and windows was no longer the safest part of the city, and Hyatt hated his beat. He would be glad when this night was over. He shuffled to the next store and rattled the windows, not turning around as the Chevy drove past him down the mostly deserted street.

The big man watched the patrolman on his rounds as he drove slowly past him and turned up the next side street. There, the long car executed a graceful U-turn and pulled to a stop at the curb. The headlights were doused, and the Chevy waited

9

in dark silence. Inside, the man in the surgical gloves and rubbers turned off the engine. Reaching for the zippered bag, he opened it and removed the gun from its plastic bag. Quietly, he rolled down the car window.

Hyatt moved slowly toward the corner of the main street, methodically doing his job. He started to cross the junction of the main street and the side street where the Chevy was parked, its driver crouched low inside, unseen from the street. Hyatt noticed the vehicle mechanically; nothing about it excited his suspicion. Yet he paused for a moment, a veteran cop looking at something that had not been there an hour before when he'd passed the spot. Automatically, he turned and took a couple of steps toward the car to check it out.

Two shots rang out into the darkness, and Hyatt caught them both full in the chest. Death took him by surprise and he hardly had a chance even to moan as he fell backward into the now-quiet street.

The Chevy's headlights came on as the car started up again. Without haste, the large car backed up the street, moving backward with as much efficiency as it had gone forward. At the corner, it turned methodically, without panic, and sped away. The man at the wheel kept his surgical gloves on as he headed toward the waterfront. His hunt was not yet over.

The neon of the bowling alley's block-long sign sent a red and blue haze upward to bounce off the darkness and obscure the stars. "Bowl-a-Rama," it said, winking lewdly. "36 Lanes," it said. "24 Hours 7 Days a Week." At the waterfront end of the sign a four-foot-high neon bowling ball eternally knocked down three pins, which tumbled perpetually, only to rise and fall once again through the magic of neon.

Three men came out of the bowling alley, laughing with masculine loudness and punching at one another's biceps. Smelling strongly of beer and the vagrant traces of cigar smoke, they discussed their scores at the tops of their lungs, punctuating their chatter with obscenities and good-natured name calling. Two of them carried canvas bags that housed their bowling balls, while the third, Johnson, pausing on the Bowl-a-Rama steps, pulled his uniform shirt on over his T-shirt. His policeman's badge was pinned to the shirt's left front, just above the row of ballpoint pens clipped inside the pocket. Buttoning his cuffs, Johnson glanced at his wristwatch dial, seen dimly in the neon's glow.

"Wow! The ol' lady'll give me hell!" he exclaimed, cursing the lateness of the hour. Johnson took his bowling-ball carrier from the man who held two and said good-bye to his companions, hurrying up the street to the parking lot where his three-year-old Plymouth was parked. He never so much as glanced at the dark Chevy that drove slowly past him, as he ducked into the lot, looking for his car. He didn't notice as the Chevy made a U-turn farther up the block and drove slowly back, past the bowling alley and into the parking lot, where it slid silently into an empty space.

Locating his Plymouth, Johnson unlocked the trunk and bent forward to stow his bowling ball next to the spare tire. As he stood upright, he heard two shots behind him but at the same second that the sound penetrated the air the bullets penetrated his brain, and the dead officer slumped forward into the half-empty trunk, the back of his head shattered.

Unhurriedly, the Chevrolet pulled out of the parking lot and into the street, disappearing around the next corner just as a small crowd emerged from the Bowl-a-Rama, drawn by the sound of the shots. By the time that Officer Johnson's body was located, the Chevy was miles away, on the other side of the city.

The used-car lot was, of course, closed for the night, its colored pennants flapping forlornly, all a uniform gray. The Chevy expertly nosed its way into the empty stall. Now it was home, in the slot from which it had been "borrowed" three hours earlier, just one more used car among all the others, its job done. Taking the zippered case from the seat, the big man, still wearing the latex gloves and the rubbers, slipped out from behind the wheel and closed the door with a firm click. Stopping in an extra-dark corner formed by the side of the lot's concrete office, he unzipped the case and slipped the now-empty gun inside. Then he stooped to peel the rubbers off his feet; next the surgical gloves from his large hands. These, too, he tucked inside the case, pulling the zipper shut with definitive firmness. Then, without looking back, he left the parking lot and the darkness swallowed him up.

Herb's all-night coffee shop was deserted at this hour. The big man looked around the counter quickly, with a professional expertise, his eyes behind their dark glasses like a radarscope scanning the place. Herb was in the back; he could hear the subdued rattle of plates being washed. A twenty-four-hour AM music-and-news station was giving the latest soft information on the Agnew case. Soon it would provide a weather forecast and then Tom Jones, for anybody still awake enough to care.

He headed for the men's room and laid the zipper case down on the washstand. Taking his coat off, he revealed a polished and worn leather shoulder holster strapped under his left armpit. The butt of a Colt .38 Special gleamed dully from the holster. The man hung his coat up on the coatrack with the care and precision that marked the way he did everything. Then he turned to the sink, rolling back the sleeves of his white shirt. He took off his dark glasses and carefully laid them down on the rim, then regarded himself in the spotted, darkened mirror over the sink.

Even in the forty-watt dimness of the men's room his face reflected the strain of the night's business. It was not the face of a killer but, rather, the face of a man who has killed. A heavy face that had once been handsome but became too beefy and florid for good looks, a face that had been under stress for too many hours between shaves. He turned on the taps and ran his hands over the bar of soap. He washed his face and neck thoroughly, taking care not to splash water on his shirt. As he reached for the paper towel, his badge clinked against the porcelain of the sink. A policeman's badge, number 206, the badge of a sergeant of detectives. Stan Boyle, plainclothesman, cop, cop killer.

Boyle came into the coffee shop from the men's

13

room, his face filmy with residual moisture. The news was still droning over the radio, a story of Arab terrorism and another hijacking. As he swung his thick leg over a counter stool, Herb, the owner and counterman, came in from the back, wiping his hands on a dishtowel, which he used to dab at the counter surface in front of Boyle.

"Oh, hi, Sarge, didn't see you come in. The usual?"

Boyle, setting the zippered leather case on the floor at his feet, out of Herb's view, merely nodded. Herb filled a glass with milk from a fresh half-pint container and set it down in front of him, adding a muffin on the side.

"Where's McQ?" he asked Boyle.

"Night off," the sergeant mumbled through muffin crumbs.

"How's the gut?" They were old acquaintances, Herb and Boyle and Boyle's ulcer.

Boyle put a hand to his stomach in an unconscious movement. "Not bad."

"Cousin of mine had half his sliced out, did I tell you? Good as new. Damn thing stretches like a lady's girdle."

Boyle, who had heard it all before and couldn't have cared less, didn't bother to answer. He glanced at his wristwatch again, as though he were waiting for something. Or somebody. He ignored Herb's casual, friendly chatter, which rose to drown out the radio news; he ignored the news, as well. Even when it turned local.

". . . The Grand Jury this afternoon returned an indictment against County Supervisor William Ry-

14

lander, alleged to have accepted payoffs for zone variances. Rylander has denied any wrongdoing and says he welcomes a full disclosure of the facts. . . ."

"They'll nail him," Herb assured the unlistening Boyle. "They should, the dummy."

Boyle, his eye on the rear counter mirror, had spotted what he was waiting for. Reflected in the glass he could see a long black sedan cruising by. The counterman, meanwhile, was having second thoughts.

"Ah, he'll get off . . . or promoted. They always do." Herb wiped his hands once more on the towel, and turned to leave the counter. "Need anything, give a holler," he urged Boyle as he headed once more for the back room and his garter-belt magazines.

Unhurriedly, as methodical in everything as he was in murder, Boyle finished his glass of milk. As the radio news segued into a big-mouth rock jock, he took some change out of his pocket and laid it on the counter. Then he took his zippered case from the floor and left the lunchroom.

Up the dark, empty streets Boyle walked, rounding a corner and approaching the parked black sedan. The front window was rolled down and, wordlessly, Boyle took the leather case from under his arm and handed it in, disposing of the murder weapon. Then, with a familiar nod to the driver, Boyle turned and started away.

He didn't get far—not very far at all. A sudden shotgun blast from the black sedan took Boyle full in the back and sent him sprawling. Nobody bothered to get out of the car to make sure he was dead.

With a sudden roar the sedan came to life and drove off, the blackness of the steel auto melting like smoke into the blackness of the night.

CHAPTER II

The steps of the Public Safety Building at First Avenue and James were crowded with officers herding in suspects like drugged steers to the slaughter. As the police car carrying Kosterman drove up and stopped, the officers in charge roughly created a single lane through the resisting flesh. With a disgusted oath, Kosterman stepped from the back seat and made his way, grimly and with distaste, through the hostile crowd of suspects, up the steps and into the building.

He was a burly man, Captain Ed Kosterman, half cop, half political animal. His thick white hair grew into a low point over his furrowed brow; the lines of his face were set into a perpetual scowl. From the neck up, he looked older than his forty-

17

five years, but his stocky body was in good trim, still more muscle than flab. Flashily and expensively dressed, Kosterman wore a tailored cashmere overcoat and a sharp fedora; on his left hand, jammed down over his hairy knuckle, a large and costly diamond caught the light, and from his wrist a solid-gold chronometer gleamed. As head of the detective bureau, Kosterman was a power in the city, and he wasn't about to let anybody forget it. Now, with two police officers dead and a third possibly dying, he was going to need every scrap of his power and energy. He made his way quickly up the stairs to Grogan's office, ignoring the questions that came at him from all sides.

Chief John Grogan was top brass, Chief of Police of the City of Seattle. Not only was this sudden rash of cop killings resting squarely on his shoulders, it was his responsibility to see that no more occurred. And it was looking like all-out war. A big, ruddy man, more a politician than policeman, he was ensconsed in an important, well-paid yet vulnerable job, the protection of which was a task in itself. Now, pulled out of a warm bed at this ungodly hour, he still wore his light topcoat as he stood at the window, intent on the scene in the street below.

It was a massive roundup; investigating officers were bringing in scores of known and suspected militants, most of them black or brown. Grogan looked down at the afros and the "naturals," at the levis and the beards and the dashikis and the army veterans' green surplus jackets. Even from several stories up, Grogan recognized a number of the black faces as being possible members of the Black Liberation Army. It looked to him as though the entire

Central District—the black ghetto—and much of the University District, with its pot smokers and hippie radicals, had been emptied and brought down to headquarters. He shrugged with annoyance and turned away from the window, damned angry at the slaying of the officers. He was pulling off his topcoat as Kosterman entered his office.

Kosterman solemnly returned Grogan's nod, and acknowledged Toms with another wordless movement of his head. Franklin Toms perched on the corner of Chief Grogan's desk, talking earnestly into the telephone. Even at this early hour of the day he appeared immaculate, perfectly groomed and dressed in the most conservative taste. A comer on the political scene, Toms was the mayor's executive aide and liaison with the police department. As an officer came into Grogan's office with wake-up coffee and donuts, Toms accepted the styrofoam cup in an elegantly manicured hand without missing a beat on the phone.

"Yes, sir . . . yes, Howard, I'm with the chief and Captain Kosterman now. . . ." Toms turned to Grogan, holding out the receiver. "Chief, the mayor wants to talk to you."

Grogan took the phone gingerly, but while his conversation with the mayor was firm, patient and guarded, he was not intimidated. "Yes, Howard," he assured, "we're on top of it. . . . Yes, I'm aware of that. No, nobody's going to get stepped on, but we're not sitting on our hands, either."

In a low tone, Toms explained the mayor's attitude to Kosterman. "He's nervous, Ed. He wouldn't like the department accused of bias."

"Bias, hell!" Kosterman exploded, careless of the

need to keep his voice down. "Frank, it's fish in a barrel! Chicago's getting one officer killing a month. New York's as bad. San Francisco. Detroit. Now it's coming our way." He waved his hand at the window, indicating the chaotic scene below. Hatred for the suspects, for the militants and the radical life styles was etched into every line of his face. "Random killings by radical revolutionaries for political purposes. . . . Not here, Frank!" He struck the desk with a furious fist. "This is a choke-off right now!"

Toms' tone was conciliatory, but his words held a warning edge. "Well, I'm a friend, Ed. You know that. But I'd be careful on this. You don't want to give the impression that the department is a law unto itself."

Hearing the warning, the political man in Kosterman took over from the cop. He brought his voice down to a casual, conversational level, and even managed a smile.

"Just doing a job, Frank. That's all. Doing a job."

McQ's apartment was a mess. It was difficult to imagine so big a mess in so small a space. The man had obviously worked hard at it, resisting the onslaughts of determined women to clean and straighten it. The attempts of fond females to build a clearing had been haphazard, occasional and short-lived. The jungle had taken over again, and the vines and tendrils of disorder curled everywhere. Old, crumpled newspapers, partly read law-enforcement journals, a few metallic, compartmented trays from frozen dinners, overflowing ashtrays, dead coffee cups with cigarette butts floating on rancid coffee like gross waterbugs. And that was only for starters. The only area of order was the wall on which a group of framed photographs was hung neatly. Undusted, maybe, but hung neatly.

In one photograph two men stood proudly side by side, grinning self-consciously at the camera. The picture carried an inscribed brass tag with the legend: "Medal of Valor Winners. Detective Partners Lieutenant Lon McQ and Sergeant Stan Boyle." In the other frames were photos of Boyle and McQ shagging a football at the beach; four laughing people sitting around a nightclub table watching the birdie. Boyle and Lois and McQ and Elaine, now his ex. And a loving if inexpert picture of a twelve-year-old, innocent-eyed girl who bore a gentle resemblance to her massive father. Any man's past.

Only one lamp burned in the darkened apartment; the phone receiver, off the hook, beeped indignantly. Ignoring it, McQ sat slumped in his undershorts, a bottle of beer in one hand and a glass in the other, from which he took deep and frequent pulls. Vacantly, he watched the blurry figures of an old movie on his TV set, which was drawn up close to his shabby, over-stuffed armchair.

McQ was a man who resembled most closely a mountain that had seen the weathering of thousands of years. A huge man, six feet five and made of stone, he had a weatherbeaten face with crags instead of features. Engraved deeply into it was a weariness borne from long years of hard, frustrating work. For, although McQ was a cop in the deepest, most old-fashioned mold, he was also a loner, a maverick with his own way of doing things. A physical man, he was a doer rather than a talker. He never trusted words. Once, with the power of a steam engine, he threw a man up onto a roof. Then he went up and threw him down again. The man was a hood. McQ knew it, but he couldn't prove it, couldn't make the charges stick. Almost crazy with frustration, McQ had let his muscles win out over his mind, and action had followed. That little caper had cost him a captaincy; the promotion had gone to Kosterman instead.

McQ stretched himself restlessly. The blue light flowing from the television set picked out the scars on the huge man's upper torso—bullet brandings. An occupational hazard, reminders of earlier wars. He glanced at the small clock next to the full ashtray. After three in the morning. If only he could sleep. He put his hand over his aching eyes, willing his entire body to sleep. But it resisted him, as he knew it would, ignoring fatigue, as restless as a nocturnal creature and as impatient for action.

He tossed the decision around in his brain awhile, then, finally, he gave in. Rising, he strode to his bathroom and began to fish through his medicine chest until he found what he was looking for. He came back into the living room with the little bottle in his hand, and shook one powerful sleeping pill out of it with a dejected sigh, downing it with a gulp of beer.

Switching off the TV, McQ pulled the blinds on the window, closing off the studio room from the neon glow outside. Then he put the phone back on the hook and climbed into bed to await blessed sleep.

The phone rang.

McQ glared at the offending instrument as it continued to ring, shattering his peace with its selfish insistence. After sixteen rings, he snatched the receiver up and growled into it. "Yeah?"

"Lon. J.C. Did you hear?"

"What?" McQ was too groggy from the pill to catch the urgent unhappiness in the voice of the young black detective.

"I'm sorry, Lon. Stan went down this morning."

The words registered, seared into McQ's brain like branding irons. His partner shot. His massive face tightened and anger appeared upon the battered features. But it was a subtle appearance; through the years McQ had learned to mask his feelings, and he did it now automatically, even though nobody was there to see.

"How bad?"

"Shotgun. In the back." J. C. too knew the value of being terse. "He's in Central Receiving. They're working on him. . . ."

McQ shut his eyes. In his mind's eye he could see the tense activity of the large hospital; could smell the emergency room at night, its odors of disinfectant and medication. J.C.'s next words brought him up short.

"Lois is here. She wants to see you."

McQ could imagine Lois Boyle, her large blue eyes twin mirrors of anxiety, worry creasing her white marble features but making her, somehow, even more desirable.

"How's she doing?" He kept his voice gruff.

"Gutsy. Holding up real well."

"What happened?"

"Don't know for sure," the young black man re-

23

plied. "No witnesses, nothing. Cafe guy heard the blast but didn't see anything."

But McQ's mind was already at work. "Pull the package for me on Manny Santiago," he ordered crisply into the phone.

J. C. hesitated, knowing this could turn into a real problem for him. "Lon, the captain won't let you in on this. You know regulations."

McQ knew regulations. They were very explicit in forbidding a detective to investigate the slaying of a partner; too much heavy emotion was involved. But that wouldn't deter him. Very much his own man, when McQ wanted to do something he did it. Simple as that.

"Get me an Intelligence update on the son-of-a-bitch," he snarled. "And I want to see Stan's log."

J. C.'s voice held a resigned acceptance of the inevitable. "Okay, fight it out with Ed," he sighed. "Lon, two other officers got taken off, too. .38s. Beat man named Hyatt, and Wally Johnson. You know, he handles the morning watch in Property. Looks like we got a war on."

McQ pondered the new information, trying to connect it to Boyle. "Yeah," he muttered, "see you," and abruptly hung up.

He sat on the edge of his bed, dressed only in his shorts, and lit a cigarette, thinking. A shot-gunned partner, critically wounded, and two dead officers killed by .38s. Was there a connection? What? His hand reached for the phone, dialed a familiar number. Dragging deeply on the cigarette, McQ listened impatiently as the phone rang again and again across town. At last it was answered by a sleepy, protesting black voice.

"Rosey, wake up and listen, it's McQ. I'm looking for anything fresh on Manny Santiago. . . ." He grimaced as the protests grew louder. "Yeah, yeah, I know he can't be touched, but"——he let the pressure show a little, steel-hard in his grating iron voice—"my partner was shot this morning. Do you understand?" He listened for a few seconds, then put a note of cajolery into his words. "You can make yourself a lot of points. Okay, but I'm in a hurry. No, I'll get to you."

He hung up the phone and switched on the lamp. As his eye fell on the bottle of sleeping pills, McQ swore. One of those damn things was inside him, slowing down his active brain and his body's powerful, trained reflexes. What to do? He couldn't go wandering around in a state of sleepiness, like a three-year-old up past his bedtime. With a deep sigh and a heavy shrug of his immense shoulders, McQ strode reluctantly into the bathroom. He stood in front of the toilet for a minute, contemplating his middle finger with a scowl. Then he stuck it forcefully down his throat, bending over the bowl and heaving until he brought up a vile mixture of TV dinner, beer and undigested sleeping pill. His face twisted in a grimace, McQ brushed his teeth hastily and climbed into his crumpled clothes, gathering them up carelessly from the chair on which they'd been thrown. Buckling on his holster, he was ready to go.

As he stepped through the doorway of his apartment building, a movement caught his eye, and McQ ducked quickly back into the shelter of the overhang, watching with narrowed eyes. On the deserted street in the predawn hour, a kid, a young punk in a tight-fitting pair of jeans and a leather jacket, circled like a panther around McQ's car, preparing to steal it.

Anyone who knew McQ even slightly knew that his car was the apple orchard of his eye. It was a sharp job, a customized special. A low-slung dark green Pontiac TransAm with stick shift, overhead cams, fin stabilizer and a souped-up engine, it also boasted dual pipes and special wide radial whitewall tires on its chrome wheels. McQ treated that car with a tenderness he reserved for nobody else on earth, except his daughter, whom he saw rarely. He washed and curried that automobile as though he were getting it ready for a cat show, and you could almost hear it purr.

Now he stood in the doorway watching some punk get ready to rip it off, a tiger watching its only cub being hassled by a hyena. Suddenly the thief made his move, starting to jimmy the door lock. An ear-splitting wail tore the night to shreds as the burglar alarm went off, scaring the punk out of his speed-freak pimples. The Pontiac was wired for sound—many, many decibels of sound.

The kid straightened up, startled out of his mind. With the alarm ringing in his brain, he turned to see McQ descending on him with the wrath of an angry tiger. He dropped the jimmy and ran like hell, McQ's long legs pounding in pursuit.

The burglar alarm on the TransAm kept wailing, sending its loud screeching into the heart of the neighborhood. Shades were pulled up and lights turned on as the people in the houses surrounding the street grudgingly dragged themselves from sleep to see what was going on. The kid, with terror in his heart, ducked like a rabbit in and out of darkened doorways, looking for a hole to hide in. In one doorway, he nearly collided with a denim-clad workman who was emerging for the early shift, carrying a lunchpail. Nimbly, the kid dodged around him and into an alley, just as McQ came roaring up behind him.

McQ headed into the dark alley after the car thief; he could see the kid sprinting furiously ahead of him. Suddenly, from some night-black hidden space, a gun cut loose, once, twice. Bullets spattered around McQ, chipping the asphalt as they headed toward him. It was a trap, with the car thief as the bait! Lightning-fast, McQ flung himself behind the meager cover of some garbage cans. The unseen gunman continued to fire, his bullets hitting the cans and making them dance around wildly, ponderous metal clowns. Silence from behind the cans: was McQ dead? The gunman evidently thought so, because, as the punk kid car thief joined him, he broke from his hiding place and both men ran from the alley.

Meanwhile, the continuous cacophonous wailing of McQ's auto burglar alarm had drawn the attention of a patrol car, which was approaching several blocks down. Seeing it, the gunman and the thief reversed their directions, heading off in the direction of the noisy Pontiac. But there they split, each running down opposite sides of the street.

Silently, McQ emerged from the alley, gun in hand. He raised his arm and held it forward, in the classic sharpshooter's stance, steady as a rock. Without haste, he took a long, careful and unhurried aim, sighting down his arm, which formed a straight line with the gun barrel. The gunman was crouched low, running swiftly forward, doubled up, using the line of parked cars as his cover. It was an almost impossible target, complicated by the dim light of the street lamps, but McQ narrowed his eyes and squeezed the trigger once.

The gunman straightened with a choked cry and fell forward to the ground, dead. McQ's unerring bullet had "threaded the needle," catching the quarry between cars and killing him instantly. Still holding the gun, McQ walked warily toward the gunman, his eye alert to movement or danger. Nothing. With his foot McQ rolled the dead man over and peered at him, trying to see who he was. The patrol car had pulled up, and two policemen were approaching, waving back the anxious neighbors in bathrobes who appeared on the street after the shots had ceased.

"Know him, lieutenant?"

McQ nodded laconically. "His name's Patty Samuels. He's no car thief, he's a hit man. He was waiting. . . . Call Homicide."

"Yes, sir."

"Tell them I'll be in as soon as I can to file a report. I'll be at Central Receiving."

One patrolman went off to radio in, while the second stayed on hand in case the lieutenant needed him. Shouldering his gun into its holster, McQ caught sight of the workman who'd been on the street all the while, witnessing the action. Before McQ's eye could catch his, the man turned hastily to go, wishing to escape involvement. But the tall police detective called after him brusquely.

"Hey, you!" McQ jerked his head in a peremptory summons.

The man hesitated, then approached reluctantly; it was evident that he was not pleased and had no wish to be drawn into the evening's business.

McQ, discovering a rip in his jacket, muttered an oath. He reached in and switched off the car alarm, then strolled to the rear of the Pontiac and opened the trunk.

The trunk of McQ's car was a conversation stopper, at least the first time anybody looked inside. What was there to say? What with stakeouts and erratic hours, not to mention his current bachelor status, McQ, in a manner of speaking, lived out of his car. Besides the mandatory spare tire, the trunk was stocked with personal objects. There were changes of clothing, for both warm and cold weather, shoes, toilet articles, electric razor, ammunition, packages of quick snacks, and more. The kitchen sink might have been left at home, but no boy scout encampment was more prepared than McQ's Pontiac for emergencies. It was an apartment on wheels. As the workman approached slowly, McQ threw his torn jacket into the mess, and selected a sport coat. Without looking at the other man, he pulled on the jacket.

"Did you see what happened?"

"You shot—" the witness began.

"Before." McQ cut him off impatiently.

"He shot at you in the alley."

"Officer," summoned McQ, "listen to this." He rummaged in the car and produced a battery operated tape recorder. Then, to the workman, he said very gently and without pressure, "Just say what happened in your own words. Start with your name and address." He held out the tiny mike.

The workman backed away, reluctant. "Look," he raised a protesting hand, "I don't want to get involved."

McQ fixed him with a look. His large, craggy face seemed to turn to steel and his blue eyes became icy probes. The workman had never seen a look of such authority, such finality. He didn't need any more convincing. "Yes, sir," he gave in meekly. As he began to tell his eyewitness story into the little mike of the tape recorder, McQ gave him a forgiving, encouraging smile, which turned to a sudden scowl as something unpleasant caught his attention. Out of the corner of his eye, McQ had spotted an empty take-out bucket of fried chicken in the Pontiac's still-open trunk. With a mighty swipe of his bearlike paw, he scooped it out and tossed it disdainfully into the nearest garbage can. He hated mess, he told himself, unaware of the irony.

CHAPTER III

It was still an hour before dawn when McQ reached Central Receiving, and there wasn't much hospital activity going on. McQ found his way to the intensive care unit, where Lois Boyle sat waiting, anxiety and fatigue making smudges under her blue eyes and turning her fair complexion to pallor. Standing at her side was an officer on duty, wordless and efficient. When she saw her husband's partner approaching, Lois stood up to greet him, holding out a tense hand that McQ took and gripped with a gentleness that almost nobody else in the world ever got a chance to see.

"How is he?"

Lois shook her dark head and the soft hair bounced on the shoulders of her wine-colored jacket. "I don't know. I'm waiting." She jammed her hands back into the jacket's pockets, unaware that the gesture pulled the cloth tightly over her magnificent breasts and slim hips. Against the anxious whiteness of her face, her hair seemed blacker and her eyes bluer than McQ had ever before seen them, and desire rose in him to color his care for Stan.

"How are you?" he asked, probing her eyes with his.

Lois forced a smile. "Don't baby me, Lon, I'm tough." Her voice cracked a little; not tough at all.

McQ, uncomfortable with the melting feeling that threatened to overcome him, was grateful for the appearance of the surgeon, who emerged from the intensive care unit still in his surgical garb. As he removed the mask from his face, the doctor caught and answered the mute question he saw on both faces.

"We call it cardiac tamponade. Bleeding in the sac that surrounds the heart. We've drained all the blood we could."

"How serious, Doctor?" Lois's voice trembled, but her words were firm.

The surgeon pulled at his lip, and decided to let her have the entire truth. A policeman's wife was expected to be strong.

"Critical, Mrs. Boyle. It depends on whether or not the leaking continues." He nodded his head when McQ asked his permission to see Stan, and summoned a nurse to escort them.

The lights never go out in intensive care; for twenty-four hours a day they glare whitely from the ceiling, giving the doctors and nurses maximum efficiency, but turning the patients into semiconscious zombies.

Stan Boyle lay pale, bloodless and unconscious against the coarse white sheets. He was surrounded by and attached to so much medical hardware that he resembled a robot rather than a human. Tubing for blood and glucose ran from bottles into his arms; he was plugged into a respirator and oxygen tank, with electrodes monitoring his heart action. He appeared to be scarcely breathing, precariously connected to life only through the coils of plastic, rubber and wire that surrounded his body.

Lois and McQ stood looking down at the unconscious man; Lon felt Lois stiffen and sag forward momentarily, and he gripped her upper arm tightly until she stood up straight. Wife and friend gazed down in silence, watching a man whose very survival was clearly a struggle of great magnitude. As the nurse shut the door behind her, leaving Lois and McQ alone with Boyle, Stan's wife spoke in a low voice.

"He liked the work, Lon. He thought being a cop was the greatest. I'm not surprised, you know. That he was shot. I've been expecting it."

McQ shot her a surprised glance. Did she know something?

"What do you mean?" he asked her gently.

"*All* wives expect it these days, don't you know that?" Lois responded with a slight shrug of her lovely shoulders. "Some crazy getting it off," she continued musingly, half to herself. "A radical doing his number. That's what the captain thinks. He was here. He told me." She turned to McQ, searching

33

his rugged face with her bright blue eyes. "What do *you* think, Lon?"

"Could be." McQ was not giving anything away, not even to Lois.

"But maybe not, huh?" The girl wasn't easy to fool.

McQ ached to change the subject. "Lois," he took her arm, turning her away from the bed, "would you like to come down and get some coffee?"

She shook her head decisively. "No. I'd rather stay here as long as they let me."

"Are you up to some questions?"

She shot him a quick, wry smile. "Police work. It never stops, does it?"

"I want to know who did this." McQ spoke very quietly, but there was no mistaking the conviction in his tone.

Lois nodded, "of course" written on her face. She walked slowly to the window and stared out, unseeing, at the night.

"What was Stan doing out last night?" McQ was gentle but persistent. "I thought he was taking you to a show. I saw him buy the tickets."

"He got a call."

"From who?"

Lois turned to face him, her brows puckered in a frown, thinking hard. "I don't know, but it was important. I saw his face. I could feel the tightness in his stomach. You know how he was, you rode with him long enough. He went right for the Maalox."

"Did you hear the conversation?"

Lois's frown deepened. "Pieces. I had a feeling

it had something to do with the drive against the dealers. Just a feeling . . . that's all. The department dries up the city, somebody tries to dry up Stan."

"Were any names mentioned?"

Lois shook her head. "Not that I heard."

But McQ was pressing hard now. "Are you sure? Manny Santiago?"

Lois nodded. "I'm sure. I'd have remembered that."

McQ drew in a deep breath, certain now that Lois Boyle had no more to tell.

"Okay," he nodded. "Lois, I've got to go. Can I call someone for you? A friend to sit with you?"

She shook her head once more, refusing help. "No, I'm fine," she assured her husband's partner.

McQ hesitated, searching for the right words. "It'll be okay," he reassured her huskily. "Stan and I'll be riding again. You'll see."

"Sure," Lois said flatly. She not only didn't believe him, she didn't even pretend to believe him.

"I'll be back as soon as I can." He looked long and searchingly at her, and she raised her face to meet the tall man's eyes. An electric glance flowed between them, its current lighting the room even brighter. McQ turned to the bed and looked at his friend, who clung feebly to the fringes of life. Then, without another word, he walked out.

As McQ approached the intensive care unit desk, he saw Boyle's surgeon filling out a report. Over his shoulder the large detective lieutenant could see the closed-circuit screens of the cardiac sentinel machines that monitored the heart action of all the patients in the unit.

"Doctor, the minute Sergeant Boyle can talk,

please call me." He reached into his wallet and pulled out his card, which the doctor took gravely.

"Certainly, Lieutenant." The doctor's eyes met McQ's. "I hope it's a call I can make."

The early sun, rising over Lake Washington, struck the waters of Elliott Bay with splinters of silver and turned the roofs of City Hall, the Federal Government buildings, Smith Tower and the Chamber of Commerce building from dark gray to dusky pink. The piers reached concrete-and-steel fingers into the waters of the harbor, and the Space Needle's futuristic shaft reflected the dawn's chill glitter. Traffic on the streets, the freeway and the Alaskan Way Viaduct was still sparse; few lights were on in the downtown office buildings. Seattle was still mostly asleep, with the exception of the street cleaners, who were out washing and brushing with fully motorized equipment. And the cops, who never sleep.

The sun bounced off the Pontiac's dark green sleek hood as McQ drove into the police headquarters garage. Moving down the ramp, he looked for a space and, finding it, nosed the low-slung car in next to the vehicles of other police officers, none of which were as sporty as the TransAm. As McQ climbed out of the driver's seat, he saw J. C. weaving toward him, through the cars, papers in his hand.

"How's Stan?" the young black detective asked.

"Hanging in," was all McQ could reply. He turned to lock his car carefully, a thing he never neglected to do, even in the police garage.

"Homicide's looking for you," offered J.C. "They

36

want your papers on the Patty Samuels thing. Captain's looking for you. I think you've got him worried." He handed McQ the material he was carrying. "Stan's log," he explained. "and the Santiago stuff."

The Santiago file was thick, and McQ flipped quickly and eagerly through it, drinking in the contents with a sharp glance. A series of mug shots came first, showing a smooth, strong man of South American lineage, gray-haired though still in his forties. Impressive-looking, even distinguished, the face in the photographs hinted of massive strength and stubbornness, of power. Santiago was not your ordinary hood, nor a bum in the lineup.

From the mug shots, McQ passed on to the Arrest and Release reports, looking for convictions. Looking over his shoulder, J. C. supplied, "All the same. Arrest for felony. Booked on misdemeanor or released. He beats them all. I guess you know how it feels."

McQ looked at the younger man. J. C. could read the rage and hatred for Santiago on Lon's face, his frustration at the department's inability to nail this man and make its charges stick. Now the hatred ran deeper, because of Stan. McQ slammed shut the file and put it back into J.C.'s hands.

"Lon, Ellen asked if you'd like to come to dinner this week. Been some time."

McQ's words were gruff. "Thank her for me, but not right now."

"Sure." J.C. could understand the reason behind the gruffness. He grinned suddenly, pointing to the car, with its black vinyl custom interior, bucket seats and other expensive optionals. "You know, that thing's an attractive nuisance. Someday somebody *is* going to rip it off. Maybe me." With a brief wave, he headed back the way he came, while McQ made his way through the garage to the basement entrance of headquarters.

Deep in the bowels of the basement was the property section, where locked doors and gates protected a warehouse full of all sorts of goods. Guns, bikes, jewelry, drugs, TV sets, and more—all stolen or confiscated articles still needed as evidence or not yet returned to owners or auctioned off. Detective Steve Dugan and the police chemist were checking in confiscated material with the police property man at the counter as McQ came in the door. McQ watched them seal the white powder in a marked and numbered manila envelope and log it in with the officer-clerk.

"Steve," he interrupted, "can you connect Patty Samuels with Manny Santiago?"

Dugan thought for a moment, his eyes narrowed. "Last rap on Samuels, Santiago's attorney handled the case."

McQ nodded his thanks for the information and then cast a quizzical look at the manila envelope being checked into Property.

"Coke," Dugan responded to the look. "Took a party up in Royal Park. Should have seen the women." He rolled his eyes upward in mock despair. "Sometimes I *know* I'm on the wrong side of the law." Then Dugan's leer faded as McQ's face reminded him. "Damn shame about Stan. Will he make it?"

McQ shrugged in silence to signify that he didn't know, turning away. The police property officer carried the manila envelope containing the cocaine deeper into the property section, into an office marked "Narcotics Room."

The room was lined with shelves. On every shelf identical manila envelopes were filed; there were literally thousands of them. Also hundreds of cardboard boxes for the larger stuff, the works and the heavy marijuana weight. It was all there: grass in keys and in j's, small stashes and dealers' lots; heroin in glassine packets; hash in dark, fragrant blocks. Morphine, coke, poppers. Uppers and downers. Quaalude. On the shelves were enough drugs to keep the entire city high, or low, depending on tastes. Stuff for swallowing, snorting, popping, chipping and injecting, for packing up your troubles in a new stoned bag. Oblivious to all this potential, the officer stowed the manila envelope on a shelf, one of the active shelves. On the shelves behind him, a sign read: "For destruction. No longer needed as evidentiary material."

McQ met pandemonium as he stepped from the elevator into the foyer. The noise was deafening and chaos seemed to be given away free. The foyer of the Public Safety Building was jammed with young men, all of them militant suspects awaiting interrogation, and all of them furiously angry and loudly vocal. Here and there, McQ spotted a handful of women radicals, even angrier than the men. Policemen and policewomen were struggling to keep order in the face of youthful rage and indignation. The officers did their best to ignore the epithets—mostly "pig" and "motherfucker"—hurled at them by the militants, most of whom were black. McQ took one look and understood immediately. The prevailing police theory on the cop killings was that militants were responsible. He scowled, watching the pushing, shoving, hostile crowd of radicals and police.

Franklin Toms, heading down an empty corridor toward the elevator, stopped beside McQ to watch the milling mob in the foyer. His suit looked as though it had just been taken from the dry-cleaner's plastic bag; his hair was perfectly combed.

"Lon, I'm sorry about Stan," he said, offering his hand. "How's he doing?"

"Trying." McQ, ordinarily laconic, became positively tactiturn around Toms.

"If there's anything I can do," it was less a question than a statement, "for him, for Lois, please let me know."

McQ merely nodded.

As he stepped into the elevator, Toms suddenly remembered, and called back over his shoulder, "Oh, captain's looking for you."

"Thanks," said McQ, turning and heading for the foyer and the pulsating mass of militants. The officers were trying to separate them, to break through their ranks and force them apart. "Come on, separate them," called one. "Captain wants them separated."

As McQ pushed through the crowd, he was intercepted and stopped by an angry young black man.

"Hey, McQ," he shouted, "what kind of asinine police shit is this? Asinine! This is illegal arrest. This is goddamn unconstitutional and you fuckin' well know it. . . ." The boy followed McQ through the crowd, shaking off the hand of a police officer who tried to stop him.

"No, let him go," McQ instructed the officer. The boy continued to follow the massive detective lieutenant, although the police officer hovered anxiously behind, obviously fearing assassination.

"Well, this whole goddamn thing is comin' down, you hear?" the boy harangued. "Man, you pigs is gonna be outta work! But shit, don't worry about it. We'll put you on welfare. That's all your fuckin' job is, anyway. . . ."

By now McQ and the boy had turned the corner from the foyer to an empty corridor, the policeman temporarily lost in the crowd behind. Alone, McQ turned to face the young black, his expression not changing one iota from the benign mask he wore.

The young militant, finding himself confronting McQ, pressed forward, close, so that his breath hissed into McQ's face as he taunted the detective.

"Go on, pig, shoot me. Pull your piece and blow me up! Right here." He drew back a little and with his daring. 'No guts, huh? You chicken-shit mother—"

The boy broke off to howl with pain. McQ, his expression exactly as it had been, one of grave courtesy, had lashed out with his incredibly long and steel-powerful leg, driving his shoe hard into the young man's shins. The boy doubled up, screaming and trying to hop on both feet at once. The policeman had by now managed to turn the corner and came running up.

"What happened?"

"He bumped into a chair," McQ assured him seriously. The officer looked around at the empty corridor. Not a chair in sight.

The cafeteria was a beehive of early-morning activity as officers and police personnel carried trays of coffee and rolls to the crowded tables. Kosterman and McQ sat facing each other across an otherwise empty table; nobody would dare approach them. A plate of ham and eggs, toast and jam sat in front of Captain Kosterman; he ate steadily and hungrily as he talked, punctuating his conversation with sips of coffee and juice. On the table by McQ's elbow sat only a cup of coffee, which the tall man ignored.

"You know how I feel about this," Kosterman was saying with his mouth full, gesturing broadly with a heavy, ringed hand.

"I saw the hallways," McQ replied.

"Garbage!" spat the police captain. "The whole building smells like rotten cheese. Christ, we'll need fumigating!" It was no secret that Kosterman detested radicals and militants and long-hairs of any persuasion.

It was no secret either that no love was lost between Ed Kosterman and Lon McQ. There was always an undercurrent of dislike between them, sometimes palpable. Those who didn't know McQ well would say that it was because McQ was passed over for the captaincy which had gone to Kosterman. But McQ himself and his friends knew better. He wouldn't say anything about it at all. Kosterman was a political man, always angling, and McQ knew why he'd been passed over. He was a loner, not an oragnization cop, a good detective but a maverick. McQ would have been a better captain, but Kosterman was a safer, more predictable one.

"Ed," McQ spoke easily, his heavy shoulders

42

leaning back against the wooden cafeteria chair, "I think we ought to be looking at something else. The whole thing's got a funny feel to me."

"I'm willing to look at anything," said Kosterman, "but uniformed officers shot on the street smells like radicals to me."

McQ didn't raise his voice. "Stan's was different," he said softly. "Different weapon. . . ."

"I know," interrupted Kosterman. "I'm not saying it's all in the same bag. Sure you don't want something to eat?" He pointed enticingly to his own greasy, yolk-smeared plate.

McQ shook his head. He wasn't a man who argued; he didn't believe much in the power of words; only actions. As always, he laid out his points. If they were picked up, fine. If not, he would go his own way.

"Ed, add in Patty Samuels unloading on me. Maybe we're looking at something we can't even see."

"Santiago?" Kosterman asked, crunching on toast.

"Why not?" McQ's tone was reasonable. "Stan and I been leaning on him. With the Feds in, his junk's pinched off. He's got to move. Maybe Stan got something and the asshole had to take him off. That'd explain the try for me, too. He'd have to assume Stan told me."

"I already thought about it," Kosterman nodded, dabbing at his mouth with a paper napkin. "I put Burt on it."

McQ leaned forward, his huge bulk looming over Kosterman. "Ed, I want it."

Kosterman looked uncomfortable; he'd been expecting and dreading this. Not meeting McQ's eyes, he intoned flatly, almost as a recitation, "No detective is permitted to investigate the shooting of a partner. Emotional involvement clouds clear judgment. You know the rules."

"I know you can stretch them," McQ remarked easily.

Kosterman shook his head. "Not this one. You're being moved into Bunco and Forgery for the time being. They want you. There's a lot of paper-hanging on the east side. . . ." He put down his fork and pushed away his plate. "Ah, that was good," he sighed, rubbing his belly.

McQ only looked at the captain; wordlessly, he rose and stood towering over him. Kosterman felt a pang of discomfort again; he knew his words hadn't gone down well with the big man. He looked up at McQ, striving for a tone of authority.

"Lon, I know you. I'm flashing you yellow. I won't stand for any breach of regulations, do you understand? So cool it. Burt's a good man. If Santiago is—" Kosterman was interrupted by the ringing phone; its peal cutting through the cafeteria hubbub. The cashier answered it, held the receiver out to Kosterman and called "Captain."

Kosterman nodded at the cashier, and turning to McQ, said, "Just a minute, I'm not through," before going to answer the phone.

"Captain Kosterman," he barked into the receiver. "No, all press inquiries go to Chief Grogan's office. Yes, the same thing goes for any lawyers. I don't want to talk to them. . . . Right." He turned to continue his conversation with McQ.

"Lon, I—" But he was talking to the empty air.

McQ had left, and Kosterman knew that he'd go his own lone way to do his own bullheaded thing. Just his style. The paunchy captain thought for a moment, then picked up the phone.

"Captain Benner, please. Internal Affairs," he told the operator. This was something he'd have to nip in the bud. And that meant now.

CHAPTER IV

Blood followed the knife. It oozed from the gory carcass onto the conveyer belt below as the long thin blade cut through fat, gristle and bone to the red muscle meat underneath. Ribs showed, heavy with beef, lightly marbled with fat, blood welling around the bone. The side of beef swayed on the hook as the razor-sharp knife boned it out. It was but one of many sides, all hanging from heavy steel hooks that fastened to a conveyor above, moving the sides slowly as a line of butchers, each wearing a blood-drenched apron, cut the beef and boned it. Huge tubs of suet stood on the floor near the belt, and the men constantly tossed fresh white and yellow fat into them. The prepared cuts were placed on the belt and carried to the various meat-processing machines.

The room was cold, very cold. It was kept at a temperature close to freezing, so that the meat would remain fresh and lose as little blood as possible; it was the blood that gave the beef its flavor. Dressed in a fur-lined jacket for protection against the bitter chill, Manuel Santiago stood apart from the butchers, looking over a checklist on a clipboard held by an employee. He turned at a quiet summons from another of his men and, with a nod, initialed the checklist quickly and turned to follow his henchman.

Santiago's private office was a large and well-appointed room; huge windows framed by long velvet drapes looked out onto the street. The thick carpet was the red-brown color of drying blood. Very appropriate. A large closed-circuit TV operation filled one wall of the room; half a dozen screens monitored plant operations. There were a number of men already in the room when Santiago entered. Among them was Bob Mahoney, his attorney.

"Hello, Bob." Santiago greeted him affably. "I thought you were in court today."

The lawyer held out his hand. "Manuel. I'm on my way. I was worried about the detective who was shot last night. I'm afraid there may be repercussions."

Santiago removed his fur-lined jacket and handed it to an assistant. Under it he wore an expensively tailored conservative business suit, in the best of taste. It fitted his tall, powerful frame well. Stepping to a mirror that hung on the wall over the mantel, he checked to see that his hair was smooth and the knot of his tie impeccable. Turning back to Mahoney, he smiled confidently.

"But why should that be?" Santiago seemed amused. "I did not shoot him. I was on a plane overnight from Mexico City."

"I'm aware of that, Manuel," the attorney replied, "but it's my responsibility to caution you about the possibility of harassment."

Santiago's smile broadened. "Ah, yes. Such a nice word. Thank you, Bob, you are very conscientious. How is he, do you know?"

"Critical."

With a long, dark finger, its nail neatly manicured, Santiago gently straightened a picture on the wall. He hated disorder. Of any kind. "Such a shame," he murmured, not troubling to hide the note of insincerity in his voice.

The phone rang, and Santiago's secretary bent quickly to answer it.

"Rio, Mr. Santiago. It's Señor Ortega."

"Thank you. Excuse me, Bob." Going to the phone, he turned away slightly and began speaking Portuguese into it. Dragging out the long telephone cord, the tall man drifted over to the window so that he could survey his empire as he talked, a sight which never failed to give him pleasure.

The Santiago Meat Packing Company was huge, a vast complex of buildings and outbuildings, of processing operations, parking areas, loading docks and giant refrigerated trucks. Around the area, workmen in white smocks moved briskly on business; more trucks, loaded with unprocessed, slaughtered carcasses, moved in a gratifying stream through the gates. Santiago ended his conversation with a smile of self-satisfied complacence. This business was a source of great pride to him.

McQ viewed the Santiago Meat Packing Company with distaste. He sat in his Pontiac, across the street from the plant, at a vantage point from the entrance. Leaning forward, the detective opened the glove compartment in the vinyl-padded dash and took out a couple of sandwiches. Picking one, he unwrapped it and took a sniff at it, as perpetually cautious as a cat faced with a new brand of catfood. It seemed okay, so he sank his teeth into it and tore off a bite. It was okay. Opening a thermos, he poured himself a cup of scalding coffee and settled down to wait, one eye on the plant and the other on Santiago's distinctive Mercedes-Benz sedan, parked in its special, priviliged spot.

It was a long wait; the two sandwiches had been long consumed and the coffee was only a memory. McQ's alert posture had yielded to a slouch and his chin was tucked into his chest, but his narrowed eyes were still glued to the packing company gates. Sooner or later. . . .

There they were. McQ sat up unconsciously. Santiago and two of his men had come out of the door to the main building and were now crossing the long cement walk to the front gates and the street. McQ watched carefully as they came out, but they didn't head for the Mercedes. Instead they crossed the street on foot, heading to a nearby steak house for lunch. McQ pivoted in the bucket seat, surveying his quarry.

Outside the restaurant a man was having his shoes shined at an outdoor stand. McQ recognized him; he was a hood by the name of LaSalle. McQ could see one of Santiago's bodyguards stopping to buy a newspaper from the vending machine; his boss and the other hood entered the restaurant. Newspaper tucked under arm, the first henchman stopped briefly at the shoe-shine stand and said a few words to LaSalle, who nodded. As he followed his boss into the steak house, McQ reached into his glove compartment and drew out an expensive Japanese camera and screwed a telephoto lens onto it. As LaSalle's shoe shine was finished and the man climbed down off the stand, McQ, still in the Pontiac, snapped a number of quick photographs. La-Salle paid the bootblack and leisurely walked away; McQ was still snapping.

McQ put the camera away and climbed unhurriedly out of his car. Automatically, he turned to lock it securely. Then, brushing the sandwich crumbs off of his wrinkled coat and trousers, he strolled casually over to the restaurant, pausing only to throw the sandwich wrapper into a litter basket, like a law-abiding citizen.

The restaurant was one of the city's finest and most expensive. Heavy cuts of beef, porterhouse and prime ribs, hung from hooks in the window, trimmed with paper frills and wearing curls of fresh parsley. McQ looked in at the window. He saw an open grill for broiling, and sawdust on the floor for atmosphere. The place was crowded, almost exclusively by men. Well-heeled men. A buffet island in the center of the large room bore huge bowls of salad makings and various dressings. There was a long line of patrons at the buffet, waiting to mix their own salads.

But Santiago didn't make his own salad.

Why should he? As he inspected the label on a bottle of wine and nodded for the waiter to open it, his two bodyguards were on line for him, one of them loading his tray with two huge tossed salads, one for himself and one for the boss. As the henchman turned away with his full tray, his attention was caught by a news broadcast over the color television set above the bar. He stopped to listen.

McQ, peering in through the window, narrowed his eyes. Why would an obedient hood keep his boss waiting while he watched a news broadcast? His puzzlement deepened as he saw the hood tear himself away from the TV and, still laden with the twin salads, hurry over to Santiago and whisper into his ear. McQ watched from the street as Santiago stood up at once and put his napkin down on the table, then hurried toward the back of the restaurant in the direction of the men's room as the first hood imparted the news to the second one, bringing him up to date on—what?

Something had definitely happened. McQ pushed open the restaurant door and entered, striding up to the bartender, who was busy with the heavy drinking lunchtime crowd.

"What was that news on TV just a second ago?" the tall detective demanded. The bartender poured a few drops of Tabasco into a shaker of Bloody Marys.

"Beats me." He shook his head.

One of the patrons sitting at the bar volunteered the answer. "The detective shot last night. He died."

Rage coursed like liquid thunder through McQ's veins, surprising even himself by its intensity. As it hit him and paralyzed him momentarily a passing customer jostled him and, stopping to apologize, froze in horror at the murderous look on the tall man's face and scuttled away. But McQ had not seen him or even felt the jostling. His head was turned, fixed on the direction that Santiago had taken. Then he looked back, checking out Santiago's bodyguards, both of whom were contentedly munching lettuce in their booth. McQ crossed the room swiftly, cutting through the crowd of waiters with his long-legged stride, heading for the men's room. As he reached it, a customer came out and quickly got out of the big man's way. McQ stepped quietly into the men's room and locked the door.

Santiago was there, speaking softly in Spanish into the phone. McQ, whose Spanish was rudimentary, could nevertheless make out what he was saying. Yes, the detective was dead. Good, it would be better for us. . . . His words were choked off suddenly as a long arm as hard as steel wrapped itself around his throat from behind. Struggling in the grip of a man he couldn't see, Santiago began to strangle and gag.

"Patty Samuels sends a message," McQ hissed in the other's ear.

"Wha . . . ?" Santiago choked for breath.

"He says he feels like shit blowing it on McQ but he rang it up with Boyle. I think you ought to send the widow a cooked ham." Savagely, McQ tightened his grip.

His face turning blue, Santiago managed to choke out in a strangled whisper, "What? Who?"

With no loosening of his iron hold on the man, McQ dragged Santiago's massive body over to face the mirror above the sink. There, Santiago could see

52

reflected his own contorted face and the savage mask of rage worn by the man who held him in a death grip. Fear tugged at Santiago's face; he had never seen McQ looking like this, like the very personification of the Furies, the mask of vengeance and death. He sucked in his breath as McQ loosened his grip to whirl him around by the shoulders, facing him.

"You are crazy!" screamed Santiago. "You are an insane man!" Burly and powerful himself, he fought to break loose from McQ's iron grip. McQ enjoyed the struggle; it gave him the opportunity to take his frustration out on Santiago, as he slammed him and roughed him up, finally shoving his captive up against the tiled bathroom wall and putting a C-clamp hold on his throat with his powerful right hand.

"Patty made a death-bed statement," he lied. "He said you put out ten grand to dead-bang on Boyle and McQ . . . ."

Santiago, unable to utter a syllable through his closed throat, shook his head "no."

McQ slammed him against the wall again, hard. "Why don't you say something?" he jeered. He slammed him again and again, slapping at the other man's face with his free hand while keeping his right hand clenched around Santiago's throat. "Come on, speak up," he encouraged sarcastically. "Do I hear a confession under duress?"

Santiago opened and shut his mouth, but no sound emerged from his battered face.

"Too bad. Never hold up in court." McQ moved in closer, putting his craggy features dangerously close to the other's frightened face. "Now listen, meatball," he hissed in murderous rage, "I'm going to get you, do you hear? I'm going to get you if it's my last move. . . ."

By the time they'd finished the last bite of salad, the boss had still not returned. One of Santiago's men was distracted by the sight of a customer trying to get into the men's room. The door was locked. Why was it locked? Suddenly alarmed, he nudged his companion, indicating the bathroom. The two men rose and hurried out of the booth, rushing across the room and reaching the men's room door just as it opened and McQ walked out.

"Never find the asshole," he remarked genially to the hoods. "I flushed him down the toilet." He strode off, with just the hint of swagger in his step.

Rushing past him into the john, the two found their boss bending over the sink, splashing water on his face. As Santiago turned to his men, they let out an involuntary gasp. The boss's face was bloody; its distinguished good looks messed up by welts, bruises, cuts and a broken nose. Now, his eyes distended with humiliation and naked fury, he looked like an ordinary hood.

CHAPTER V

It was the smallest package she ever remembered holding, just an envelope and a small paper bag. Her husband's personal possessions; all that was left of Stan Boyle.

"Thank you," Lois Boyle said to the nurse. She turned to see McQ coming down the lighted corridor. He stood by her side, looking silently at the pitiful little bags she held, then took them from her hands and led her away from the nurses' station, a gentle hand on her arm.

They didn't say a word to each other in the elevator, or on the hospital steps or as McQ led her to his car. He unlocked the door and handed her in on the passenger side. As he bent to slide under the wheel, a patrol car drove up and a uniformed officer approached McQ.

"Captain Kosterman wants to see you."

"I'm taking Mrs. Boyle home."

The officer looked pained; he hadn't requested this chore and didn't want it. "Lieutenant," he insisted, "he wants to see you *now*."

McQ looked him full in the face so that there would not be the smallest possibility of misunderstanding. And he spoke each word clearly and distinctly, as though addressing a very young child, while the police officer winced.

"I'm taking Mrs. Boyle home." Then he got behind the wheel. Kosterman would be madder than hell, he thought with an involuntary grin.

Kosterman *was* madder than hell. He strode down the hallway next to McQ, conscious of the fact that he had to take two steps to keep up with each of McQ's single strides, and that he looked ridiculous, almost running beside the tall detective.

"Christ," he swore, "the phones haven't stopped ringing! Upstairs, City Council, the Mayor's office. The man has clout. What did you expect, his lawyer was going to let it die?"

"I never touched him." McQ lied with ease.

Kosterman stopped dead in the corridor and glared up at McQ.

"We talked," McQ continued easily. "Sure. He slipped on the wet floor and fell against the sink."

"*His* version is otherwise," shouted the captain. "And so is his men's."

McQ shook his head in mild amusement. "But they weren't there," he pointed out reasonably. "We

56

were alone. Besides, they're his men. They lied."

As they approached the conference room, Kosterman shot him a look that said plainly that he didn't believe McQ. But he knew that the flimsy story would be McQ's "defense," and that he would stick to it. He uttered a sound of disgust as he turned the knob on the conference room door and preceded McQ inside.

McQ glanced around at the heavy array of brass in the large room. Seated around the conference table were Chief of Police Grogan, Franklin Toms and the police commissioner. It was evident to McQ that "court" was in session and that, furthermore, the verdict had already been brought in although the defendant had just arrived.

"You're off investigation, Lieutenant, pending review," barked Grogan.

McQ looked around at the grave, closed faces in the room; their minds were evidently made up. What could he say? He was a man who had little faith in words, anyway.

In his cool, undersell way, McQ began. "Santiago is the biggest dealer in the city, despite all his cover. Intelligence knows it, the Feds know it. His H comes down from Canada by mule; his coke comes up from South America stashed in meat. Nobody's been able to make it stick. Okay, his inflow's under pressure. He's got to find a new supply or some other dealer steps in and puts the grease under him. I think it's possible Stan tipped to something—"

The police commissioner interrupted, "File your report, Lieutenant. The commission will be pleased to consider anything you have to say. A date will be set for the review board. You will be notified." The dry tone was final.

"That's it," echoed Grogan. "Until further notice, you're on a desk."

McQ turned to look at Kosterman, who spoke up defensively. "I warned you, Lon. You'll be lucky if you get back on a patrol car."

McQ nodded; words had proved useless, as he'd known they would. He stood silent for a beat, then made up his mind. Without a word he began to shed the tools of his profession. On the polished wood conference table he placed his I.D. card, then his handcuffs and his service revolver. Instantly the other men knew what McQ was doing.

"Lon, don't do it," Toms said with sympathy in his voice. "Think about it. You've got a lot of years in, a fine record of arrests and convictions. . . ."

"Frank, let him go," put in Kosterman, unable to hide his relief. "He's not part of the department anyway."

McQ let his eyes meet Kosterman's, and saw the gleam of triumph dancing there. With a small smile, he brought out his badge and waved it at the captain.

"Here," he offered. "Take it and go with it." He rang it down on the table like a half-dollar, with a contemptuous toss, then turned and left the room, no longer a detective lieutenant.

J. C. picked up McQ outside the door and moved down the corridor with him.

"What happened?" the black man asked.

McQ didn't answer. Instead, he withdrew a roll

of film from his pocket and handed it over to the younger man.

"Run this through the photo lab for me, will you? See if you can get me a make. I'll call you."

"Lon. . . ." J.C. put out his hand to stop his friend, but McQ was gone, out the door and down the steps, leaving J.C. to stand looking after him, a puzzled and anxious look on his face.

He had a clean shirt on and was looking for his jacket when the door buzzer sounded. McQ opened the door without asking who it was; Lois stood there, looking very vulnerable and tired in the dim light of the apartment-house hallway.

"I hope you don't mind," she said with a small smile. "I just couldn't sit home."

McQ pulled her inside. "I was going to call you anyway." He studied her for a minute, not liking what he saw. "You all right?"

"Yes. . . . No, but let me fake it. The funeral's Tuesday morning. Come hold my hand."

"Of course."

"City's making a big thing of it. A triplet. Fifty motorcycles. Lots of media coverage. I'm sure—Christ, why does anybody want to be a cop?"

She was tense, rambling, very untogether, but McQ let her go on, being gentle with her, as one treats an extremely fragile piece of precious porcelain.

"I'm glad now we had no kids," Lois said with a sob in her voice. "Maybe it would have been better though, having someone. Who knows?" Suddenly aware of the way she was acting, she looked

59

searchingly at McQ. "Lon, you don't mind this, do you?"

"No."

"Do you have a drink around?" She tried a small smile, but failed.

"Sure."

He went for the bottle and found it, but finding a clean glass wasn't in the cards. Finally, he settled for a dirty one, and carried it out of the kitchen to find Lois drifting around the room, unable to settle in one place or sit down, restless and nervous. He made a rueful face at her, meaning the glass, and she smiled reassuringly.

"That's all right. Alcohol purifies."

He smiled back at her and shook his head, then went to wash a couple of glasses. Over the rush of water, he could hear Lois's voice.

"How do you stand it, this boil-in-a-bag living?"

"Not so bad," he called back, drying the glasses. "Soda? Water?"

"Doesn't matter. Why don't you get a woman, Lon? At least she'd straighten up for you."

He faced her in the doorway with a smile. "You forget. Women's Lib. That's not enough for them anymore."

Lois smiled back. "No, and I agree." Her eye fell on the photograph of McQ's daughter, and she went closer to examine it. "Growing up, isn't she? Still do the Sundays?"

"Wouldn't miss it." It was the good part of his life, seeing his daughter.

"Why should you? You have something good, keep it." She passed on to the posed and smiling photograph of the foursome in a nightclub. "I remember that," she said. "Vegas. It was fun."

"Long time ago." He handed the drink to her.

"Thanks," she said. Then, seeing his empty hand, "You?"

"Not right now."

"I saw Elaine in the papers," Lois continued. "She and Forester at some kind of lawyer's meet. He sure got up there all of a sudden."

"I'm glad for her," McQ said without bitterness.

Lois looked at him sharply, trying to read him, trying to determine if he had any lingering feelings for his ex-wife. But McQ was giving nothing away but drinks. Acting cool, he changed the subject.

"Lois, what are you going to do?"

"Clean things up around here. Look for a job. Maybe drive down and spend some time with my folks. I haven't told them yet. What's the point?" She turned suddenly to face him, turning her large, moist blue eyes up to his own. "Lon, can I be your sister?" she asked.

"Why not?" He smiled a crooked smile at her; it touched but one corner of his wide mouth.

"Then let's do something crazy, brother. Wednesday. Let's get in your car and go someplace. Canada. Get lost for about ten years. Ten years sounds just about right."

Suddenly she was crying, great racking sobs that sent the tears pouring down her cheeks and neck. Her hold on herself finally gone, Lois broke down and cried loudly, almost wailing in her grief. At first McQ watched her sympathetically, not interfering. Then, after a bit, he did go to her, taking a clean handkerchief from his pocket and handing it to her; standing very close to her, he forbore touching her. Finally she began to come out of it, the sobs giving way to silent weeping and then to sniffles and nose blowing.

"It's all right, isn't it?" She meant the tears.

"Sure." He meant everything.

She dried her cheeks and eyes, and tossed back her cloud of black hair. "All over," she said. "Well. What about you? I heard you quit."

"Yes."

"Surprise. I thought you were on the conveyer belt forever. I always saw you as a compulsive cop. What the Lone Ranger would have been like if he'd fought dirty."

Her metaphor made him smile. Crossing to his coat closet, he opened it and moved his body to block the closet from Lois's view.

"Well, congratulations," Lois continued. "Nothing lost. The creeps have made all the gains. The cops get to listen to a lot of organ music. . . ."

Unseen by Lois, McQ removed a revolver from the closet shelf and shoved it into his belt, under his jacket.

"Go get yourself a good job," she advised him.

"I've already got one," McQ replied.

Lois looked at him, puzzled, unable to guess his meaning, but knowing he had one, as McQ was not a man to spend words in small talk.

"Lois, I'm sorry," he said gently, touching her lightly on the arm. "I've got an appointment. Can I drop you at a friend's?"

Mystified, Lois Boyle made no protest, but picked

up her purse and let McQ lead her gently from his apartment. She sensed a tension in his touch and for the moment she was content not to ask why.

CHAPTER VI

Near the Civic Center there are a clutch of two-story buildings that house bail bondsmen, shyster lawyers, cheap accountants, and the like. In one of those buildings, two offices claimed one floor each. On the ground floor, as the sign indicated, was a bail-bonds office boasting twenty-four-hour service, "fast, confidential." On the floor above, the top floor, the window proclaimed, "Edward M. Farrow, Private Investigation."

Pinky Farrow leaned back in his wooden chair and appraised McQ. An old-time, former cop whose violent red hair had faded to sparse gray, Pinky's limp, acquired in the line of duty, still remained with him. Now a private dick, Pinky eked out a modest living in a small two-room office. Outside, in the single outer room, he had a receptionist, a file clerk, a secretary-typist and a girl who made the coffee. But for all these jobs, he paid Edith only one salary. In his own modestly appointed inner office, Pinky kept a desk and a couple of chairs, and a small refrigerator that held Edith's milk and his own cans of beer. He set the legs of his chair back on the floor with a thump, looking McQ in the eye.

"Missed you at the poker game, Lon. What happened?"

"Got tied up. You know how it is."

Pinky nodded. He knew how it was. "Can I get you something?" he offered. "Coffee? A beer?"

McQ shook his head. "No, thanks." He got right to the point. "Pinky, I want to come in with you."

The older man pursed his lips and narrowed his eyes. "So that's what it is. I wondered. Lon, there's hardly enough for me. Some door-shaking, bad checks. Even divorce has gone sour. Dissolution is putting me out of business. The lawyers don't like it. What about us?"

Shaking his head and smiling, McQ answered, "No salary. I want the cover of your license. I haven't got time to have an application processed. I want a base. I'll pay for the space. I'll even bring in my own client."

"Who?"

"Me."

Pinky nodded. "I see. Stan. Do-it-yourself gumshoeing. How come?"

"Kosterman's brains are stuck on radical revolutionaries," McQ explained. "Maybe it's a good move politically. I don't think the whole answer's there."

"Where?" Pinky was as laconic as McQ, which

was probably the main reason the two men got along so well.

McQ shrugged a don't-know-for-sure shrug. "It's some kind of scramble," he said. Maybe Manny Santiago. . . ."

Pinky nodded again. "Well, everyone to his own hangups. But, Lon, why quit? Why don't you just take a leave?"

"It's freer this way."

The old man thought for a moment, then came up with a telling argument. "Lot of bad asses on the street carrying your bruises. They'd love to see you out there without the department umbrella. You won't last."

But McQ was nothing if not a fatalist. He never bothered his head with probabilities, only certainties. "Part of the bundle. . . . How about it?" He looked at Farrow earnestly, hating to beg.

Pinky gave in with reluctance. "If it's what you want. Let's go over, I'll get you registered. Jeez"— he gave a small, apprehensive chuckle—"will Kosterman get hot!"

McQ entered the Public Safety Building for the first time as a civilian, ignoring the curious looks that followed him and Farrow. The fingerprinting went quickly, the first part of the licensing application. His hands still bearing faint traces of the ink pad, Lon stood next to Pinky as the older man filled out the necessary forms, which he shoved over to McQ.

"Sign there, Lon."

As McQ bent over the papers, he caught a glimpse of Kosterman. The captain stood in the doorway, next to the police officer who had evidently informed him. He knew what McQ was doing and it didn't make him happy. Kosterman's nostrils flared in anger and his jaw muscles jumped beneath the skin, but he said nothing, only turned and strode off, with the officer following anxiously. Lon bent to the forms again, signing into life his new career.

"His name's Freddie LaSalle. He's a contract man from St. Louis." The three men—McQ, Pinky and J.C.—stood looking at the photographs of the man on the shoe-shine stand, McQ's photographs that the police lab had processed. Around them, traffic flowed heavily, downtown Seattle in midday. They were taking their lunch *al fresco,* at the hot dog stand four blocks from headquarters.

J. C.'s identification startled McQ, and he bent closer to better inspect the photographs.

"How'd he get past the airport watch?" he queried.

J. C. shrugged. "Drove in. Who knows?"

"Surveillance on him?"

"Would be," J. C. agreed, "if we could find him."

"What about Intelligence?" McQ demanded. "Why's he here?"

"Nothing."

"Okay. I'm located now—Pinky's. You've got the number?"

The young black man nodded. McQ, stepping into the pay phone on the corner and dropping in his dime, said to J. C. over his shoulder, "I'm counting on you to keep me up on things."

"I'll do what I can, Lon, but my neck goes out only so far," warned J.C.

McQ nodded agreement, dialing. "It's the only

way." Then, into the phone he said, "Rosey, it's me. How about it? Turned up anything for me?" He frowned at the click, incredulous. Rosey had hung up in his ear.

Pinky Farrow shook his head with a wry smile. "None of your snitches'll do you much," he said. "They know you can't deal anymore."

McQ remained unperturbed. "There are ways," he replied evenly, hanging up the phone.

The neatly manicured and frequently watered lawn stretched from the stone house down to the street. McQ sat in his car observing the house. Expensive, with two storys and lots of trees and shrubs and flowers out front. Rose bushes in full bloom. It was obviously the house of somebody very much on the way up, if not already there. In the driveway and around the front of the house, a number of '74 automobiles were parked, many of them luxury jobs, like Cadillacs and Lincolns. McQ sighed. It was evident that he was wishing he didn't have to do whatever it was that he had to do. Slowly, reluctantly, he got out of the Pontiac.

He started up the lawn to the front door, but his attention was drawn by party sounds coming from the side of the house and he directed his steps to the side gate instead.

A garden tea was taking place, and the guests were all women. The beautiful rear garden, richly in flower, made the perfect setting for the afternoon party and the colorful summer frocks of the guests. The swimming pool glistened an impossible chemical blue, and the tennis court beyond put the finishing brush stroke on the portrait of affluence. McQ stopped as he saw a servant coming through the gate, carrying cakes on a silver tray.

"Henry, tell Mrs. Forester I'd like to see her, please."

"Yes, Lieutenant." Discreetly, the butler sought out a woman chatting in a group near the pool. Excusing herself, she came forward to greet McQ. Blond, in her thirties but looking some years younger, Elaine Forester, McQ's former wife, was a very good-looking woman, almost a knockout. She was expensively but tastefully dressed and McQ's hands suddenly itched to stroke and disarray that stylish hairdo of hers.

"Lon . . . this is a surprise." It was obvious that she was not without feeling for him, either.

"Elaine," he greeted her, taking her outstretched hand. "Nice party."

Elaine waved an elegant red-tipped hand in a deprecating gesture. "We're trying to raise some money for a foster-parent program." Her gray eyes searched for Lon's. "Awful about Stan. I tried to reach Lois. I'll keep trying." She paused for an instant, then said, "I heard you resigned."

"Yes."

"I'm glad," she said impulsively. Then, "I'm sorry, too . . . that it didn't happen long ago."

Their eyes met in a long look. Her implication was clear, and he got her message. Had he resigned long ago, their lives might have been very different. McQ understood Elaine very well; he knew that her rejection of him was not of himself as a man but of his way of life and the perils of his work. He bore her no grudge.

"Ginger still in school?" he asked.

"She'll be home any minute."

Never one to mince words, McQ stated his business plainly and at once. "Elaine, I need five thousand dollars."

Surprised at his request, she stared at him, eyes wide. When he didn't continue, she pulled herself together with a light laugh. "I hope it's for a woman. Someone patient, brave and caring who doesn't break out in rashes at being left alone at night." Her tone changed abruptly to a businesslike one. "I'll have to ask Walter."

McQ nodded. Of course.

As if on cue, Walter Forester came up the lawn looking for his wife. He was tall, although not as tall as McQ, and some years older than Elaine. He carried himself well; his body was trim and fit under his blazer, and he walked with the assurance of someone who has it made.

"Darling, did you happen to see my brief on the — Oh, hello, Lon."

"Walter." McQ inclined his head politely; he bore Forester no grudge, either.

"Well, you're looking fit," Elaine's husband complimented.

"You too," replied McQ.

"How about Elaine?" There was a note of proud possessiveness in Forester's voice as he put his arm firmly around her waist to let McQ know whose she was now. "Looking marvelous, isn't she?"

"Always did." McQ meant it.

Elaine turned to her husband. "Walter, Lon wants five thousand dollars."

"Loan," McQ explained. "I've got seven or eight

in pension, but it'll take a month or so to get it. I need the money now."

"All right," Forester said without hesitation. It pleased him that McQ had to come to him for money. It pleased him even more that Elaine had witnessed the event.

"Draw up a paper," said McQ. "Have the fund release the money directly to you."

"That's not necessary," Forester said expansively. "Pay me back when—"

"No," McQ interrupted him. "I'd like to do it that way."

Forester nodded his agreement. "I'll get you a check," he said, turning to the house. Just then, a private-school bus drew up in front of the driveway, and a bouncy, preadolescent girl climbed down, clutching her books to her chest and turning to wave at her friends. McQ's face lit up with tenderness, as it always did at the sight of his twelve-year-old daughter, Ginger.

Running up the lawn, the girl spotted her father. "Daddy," she yelled with joy, and sprinted toward him. He swooped her up in the air and hugged her close.

"Hi, Mom!" Ginger called from the circle of McQ's arms. "Wow, look at this!" She exhibited a test paper with pride. "Ninety-nine out of a hundred. I'm a genius," she whooped. They stood there laughing, the three of them—mother, father, child— as though the word "divorce" had never existed. Then the mood broke.

"Honey," McQ said to Ginger, "how about a basketball game Sunday? I've got two tickets."

Ginger looked at her father mournfully. "Gee,

Janie invited me to their house at the marina! It's her birthday! She's having a boy-girl party! My first one!"

McQ felt a strange pang, which he hastened to repress. Boys! He understood; it was the true beginning of the father-daughter separation, the birth of the young lady who is aware of her powers. "Well," he said gently, "you better go to Janie's. We'll do it next week."

"If there's not another party," Ginger cried gleefully. "I'm getting very popular, you know," she said with mock pomposity. "I think it's my charm!" The three laughed again, happiness restored.

At that moment, Forester came back out of the house, waving the check for the ink to dry. Handing it to McQ, he said, "I'll phone the bank and tell them you're coming down to cash it. There won't be any difficulty."

"Thank you, Walter, you're a nice fellow." McQ meant it sincerely. He bent down to give Ginger another kiss and a long, loving hug, his eyes meeting Elaine's anxious ones over the top of their daughter's head. Then he waved and walked away without another word, leaving his daughter and his wife with their new protector.

Night is kind to the streets of the Central District, shadowing the garbage and the rats, and hiding some of the shabby poverty under a blanket of darkness. Kind to the streets, but cruel to the people, keeping them indoors, with windows locked and doors bolted. At night the streets were given over to nocturnal prowlers, some two-legged, some four-legged. Allie was one of these, a junkie and a badass, always looking for some spare change for a fix, not caring much about what he had to break to get it. He was walking the streets now, but he was reasonably cooled out. Because he was on the nod, floating off in a world white with powder, dreaming of pieces of scag.

"Allie . . ." McQ spoke softly, coming out of the darkened doorway and falling into step beside him.

"Oh, hi, Lieutenant. Hey, I hear you're not the Man anymore."

"Not true, Allie." Friendlylike. "Don't believe everything that's put out." He took the junkie by the arm and led him into a lighted doorway filled with shadows. He peered into the darkness, deep into Allie's eyes.

"Your eyes are coming down," McQ said in mock sorrow.

"No, shit!" Allie protested. "Shit, Lieutenant, I'm not on it. Honest! Just a little sleepy, that's all. Been workin' hard. . . ."

"Let me see your arm," ordered McQ.

Allie pulled up his sleeve, revealing a needle crater the size of a silver dollar in the crook of his elbow, and a tracking of criss-crossed marks.

"Scratches, that's all," he assured McQ. "Bug bites, know what I mean?"

"Been shooting your tongue?" McQ wanted to know.

"What? No!" The boy poked out his tongue and folded it up for inspection. "Look! I wouldn't do that!"

McQ ignored the tongue, but spoke with mock seriousness. "Yeah, you're on the nod all right.

Bad. I hear you're stepping up, too. I hear you're pushing now."

"No! Jesus, that's illegal." The junkie cowered back from McQ's gaze.

"That's what I hear." McQ nodded solemnly. "You're carrying dirty."

Allie began to sweat. "Personal, that's all," he babbled. "Chippin', just a little chippin', I swear. . . ."

McQ straightened up to his full six feet five, and the junkie, a foot shorter, quailed. "Well," said McQ, "I'll let it go this time, but tell me something. Where's Rosey?"

Hearing the price of the ticket home, Allie's knees almost gave way under him. But he knew that what McQ wanted he took by any means, so he gave him what he wanted.

And now McQ was ready to roll.

CHAPTER VII

The harness-racing grandstand was crowded with men and women out for a good time, to pass the summer night yelling and cheering and winning or maybe losing—surely losing—a few bucks. With an expertise borne of many years' experience, McQ scanned the huge crowd, his trained eyes narrowed to pick out exactly what he was looking for.

And Rosey was never hard to spot, even in a mob like this one. A tall black man who habitually wore the latest, baddest vines, tonight Rosey was a vision in a long black velvet coat topped by a fluffy fur collar. On his large head he sported a matching velvet hat that trailed a long, plumelike feather; and on each arm he wore a flashy young fox, also dressed to the gold in their teeth. One of his girls was black, big-breasted and high-rumped in a cling-ing dress; the other, the white girl, boyishly slim and looking no more than fifteen. McQ, lounging against a grandstand pillar with a folded newspaper tucked under his arm, watched the fly trio move toward the hot-dog counter for refreshments. As Rosey bit into his dog and sipped beer out of a wax-lined cup, McQ eased in next to him.

After one long contemptuous stare, the black man turned his back on McQ, deliberately ignoring him, and moved down the counter to ostentatiously spread more mustard on his dog. McQ moved down after him, not saying a word. The black man whirled.

"Hey, man," he cried indignantly, "I don't have to talk to you. You're not heat anymore. Know what I mean? You're useless!"

McQ said nothing in reply. Rosey's attitude was, after all, hardly unexpected. The snitch paid strict attention to the spreading of the mustard, fastid-iously making certain that the goo reached every corner of the roll.

"So, hey, whatta you gonna do?" Rosey chal-lenged. "Go fist-city on me? Shit, I can use a week in the hospital for the rest and relaxation."

McQ spoke for the first time, easy, sure. Not sweating it. "Rosey, I've got five bills folded in this newspaper. . . ." He knew that money was the way to this man's tongue.

"Man, I won't fart for less than ten. . . ." Rosey giggled. He preened and grinned for the benefit of his ladies; it was something new for him to have McQ's nuts in a cracker, and he was enjoying seeing the big man burn. McQ's eyes were slits and his mouth tightened so that the muscles in his jaw jumped, but he kept his voice easy and nice.

"Okay," he agreed finally. "*If* it's beautiful."

There was a pause while Rosey sniffed at the proposition and made up his mind. Deciding it was worth it, he turned away from the girls, out of their hearing, speaking low to McQ.

"Santiago's got company. Out of state."

"Freddie LaSalle," snorted McQ, disgusted at the old news. "That's worth zip. I'll keep the newspaper. Enjoy the races." He turned to go, but Rosey's words held him there.

"Yeah, LaSalle's one of them. But there's more hardware. German Karl from Denver."

McQ was puzzled now, his interest held. "Two hit men?"

"Three," said Rosey. "Lou somethin'-or-other from Miami."

"Santiago's collecting a murder squad?"

"Somethin' else," said Rosey, going all the way.

"What?"

Rosey paused, significantly silent. McQ understood the reason and dug down deep, reaching into his coat pocket for his wallet, counting bills and slipping them into the folded newspaper.

"Heist team," said Rosey, satisfied.

McQ exploded in disbelief and anger. "Hit man for a heist? Rosey, you're shining me on . . ."

But the black man shook his head in denial. He was positive of his information. "No, it's the straight skinny. Must be somethin' special. . . ."

"Drugs?" asked McQ.

Rosey shrugged. "You tell me, what's Santiago's bag?"

"Did Stan find out about it?" McQ needed to know.

The snitch shrugged again. "He had his connections. Ask them."

McQ paused, sifting, sorting, filing and storing this heavy information for evaluation. Overhead, the squawk of the P.A. system announced the start of the next race.

"Hey, man," protested Rosey, his pink palm turned upward, "I'm missing the action."

"Rosey, if this is a shine, I'll come back and iron your face." He put the newspaper down on the counter and started away.

The black man caught at his sleeve. "I think it's worth more," he demanded.

McQ shook off the hand as easily as a fly. "I owe you some blue chip stamps."

Clustered together in the back streets of the downtown city were a group of cheap, seedy hotels. Never first-class, they had now so descended into rundown ugliness that their walls had long forgotten what ordinary, decent people looked like. Their halls were now the haunts of addicts and cheap pushers, way, way down on the social scale of dealing, purveyors of nickel, dime and quarter bags. Sleazy whores rented their rooms by the half-hour, and never stayed the full time. Old welfare clients, degraded and oppressed into early senility, lived like ancient roaches in the cracks of the hotels. The whole section was, in a word, funky.

Sal, low-down pusher of small weight, dealer in quarter bags, came out of the doorway of the Excelsior Arms and started down the street. Sal was so naturally furtive in appearance that it was hard to tell whether he was really on the lookout. Today, apparently, he wasn't, because as he crossed the next alley an arm reached out and dragged him in with a quick yank.

Sailing across the alley and bouncing off the far wall, Sal scrambled to his feet and started to run. As he dashed away, he put his hand into his pocket and transferred something to his mouth. But McQ was after him like lightning and grabbed him again, shoving him up against the wall, gripping his throat with one hand in that C-clamp grip that he'd used on Santiago, the grip that was the big man's trademark.

Choking and gagging, Sal tried desperately to swallow, but against his will and unable to do otherwise, he only succeeded in spitting up the saliva-covered contents of his mouth. McQ's free hand produced a handkerchief, which he held under Sal's mouth, grabbing the little colored balloons as they popped out, one by one. Three small, innocent, child's balloons. Each filled with twenty-five dollars' worth of cocaine.

Having gotten what he wanted, McQ released his grip on the small man's throat. Rubbing his neck vigorously, Sal the Pusher squeaked a protest.

"Hey, what the hell is this? You ain't even no cop anymore."

McQ shoved two tickets into Sal's pockets. "Here, go to a basketball game," he urged. Nobody could ever say that McQ didn't pay for what he took.

The taxi pulled to a stop outside the small court-yard of bungalow apartments. Wrestling with her packages, Myra got out awkwardly, her slim legs skittering under the heaviness of the bundles and the extra weight she was carrying on her body. Paying the driver and rearranging the packages for better balance, she made her way through the courtyard to her own bungalow, and turned the key in the lock.

It was dark, just as she'd left it. Myra kicked shut the door and snapped on the light. Turning from the door, she let out a gasp. McQ was sitting quietly in one of the overstuffed chairs, a handkerchief bunched on his lap.

Narrowing her eyes, Myra began to scold. "Jeez, you've got a lot of nerve pickin' your way in. What is this? I've got a good mind to call a cop!"

Wordlessly, McQ spread open the handkerchief, revealing the three colored balloons. The sight of them took Myra's breath away; she was no stranger to the package or its contents. But she struggled to maintain her cool, to prove her indifference. She forced a shrug, and a negligent lift of her eyebrows.

"So what?"

"Thought you might be interested," McQ replied laconically, his hawk eyes never leaving her plump face.

"Why should I? I'm no doper," she lied. "Where'd you get that idea? Look, I'm tired. I've been hustlin' drinks for ten hours. My feet hurt, my back hurts and I need a bath. Now go on, blow." But even to her own ears the words sounded hollow and her tone lacked conviction. She headed for the bedroom to change out of her high heels and girdle.

Looking at herself in the mirror, Myra frowned

in vexation. What she saw didn't please her. It might have been worse, but once, years ago, too many years ago, it had been a lot better. She peered at herself in the glass, at the coarseness of her complexion ill-masked by the caked powder that gathered in the seams along her nose. With dismay, she studied her double chin and the gray roots of the hairs around her temples. Disgustedly, she pinched at the roll of flab around her thick waist. With something like despair, Myra kicked off her shoes and began to change out of her work clothes.

Rising from his chair, McQ strolled over to the closed bedroom door. He needed Myra, needed her badly. She was one of Stan's "connections," and he had to know what she might know. But the way to Myra was with honey, not brute force. So, very carefully and in his most gentle tones, he said through the door, "Myra, let's cut through it, huh? You've been a good friend to Stan in the past."

Myra jerked her chin up as she pursed her lips in a pout. "Well, he was a nice guy. He was a gentleman." Her attitude told McQ very plainly that Myra found him *not* a gentleman. "Gentleman," she said softly, crashing on the memory of Boyle's death. "It's a goddamn shame. Oh, not that there was anything between us. Personal, I mean. We were just friends." She preened a little bit, hoping McQ would think she was lying.

The picture of Lois Boyle, of her slender, vivid beauty flashed across McQ's brain, and he contrasted that picture with the coarse and aging woman before him. "Sure, I know that," he said softly. "He respected you."

"You bet he did," Myra retorted with a toss of her head.

"He brought the balloons and you . . . spoke . . . about things in general," McQ prompted.

Myra bristled, defensive about her informing. She was no common snitch, no ordinary police stoolie. "I hear something, it's my civic duty to mention it in the proper place. Jeez, who else knows? Why don't you guys print up a program?"

McQ shook his head reassuringly, even though she couldn't see it. "Nobody knows, Myra. But I was his partner."

Myra came back into her dingy living room. She had fluffed her hair out around her face and put on a clean chenille robe, from which her astonishingly slender ankles peeped, trim vestiges of earlier years.

"Well, I only talked to Stan and *not* his partner. I'm not talking to you. I don't like you, I never did. You're a bear; I don't like bears. Out."

McQ carefully folded the handkerchief over the balloons and stowed it in his pocket, then turned and headed for the door.

"Wait a minute," Myra called out, vexed and indecisive. "Scag or coke? I don't go scag."

"I know that, Myra." His voice still held that pampering note, as though speaking to a beloved and very spoiled child.

"Can I see one?"

Producing a balloon from the handkerchief, McQ handed it over. Myra opened it carefully, and examined it. Cocaine. She looked at it for a beat, then pulled a mirrored tray off the table and spread the powder out with care, arranging it in two thin lines on the hard, nonabsorbent surface. She glanced slyly at the tall man.

"Happen to have a bill handy?"

Obligingly, McQ took out a hundred-dollar bill and waved it at her.

Myra nodded. "C-note," she murmured in appreciation. "Class. Roll it for me like a good fellow, will you?"

Rolling the bill into a thin tube for snorting, McQ watched Myra turn down the lights in the room.

"Do you mind?" she asked rhetorically. "Hard on my eyes. You see, the lounge is dark all the time so my pupils get dilated. Dilated pupils is a natural condition with me. Which makes *some* people think I'm a coker." She clicked on the radio, and hard-driving rock came blaring into the room.

"Myra," McQ purred, "did Stan have some information? Is that why he was killed?"

But Myra's eyes were busily ranging over the tall man's massive, rock-hard body. She was getting to like McQ, more and more every minute. "Why don't you take off your coat," she cooed. "Aren't you hot? Personally, I think it's hot."

"Myra," McQ persisted, "do you know anything about a drug heist?"

"You think I'm fat?" she pleaded, stroking her heavy body with her plump fingers, watching McQ's face for a morsel of praise.

"No, I think you look real nice," he lied.

She gave a small, embarrassed but pleased laugh. "Yeah . . . aw, I'm fat. Baby fat." And she giggled cutely, pleased with her wit. She looked at her reflection in the mirror on the wall, and frowned as she patted her chin. "Christ, it needs liftin'. Even that won't help. It needs a complete overhaul."

McQ tried to keep it together. "Myra," he whispered, "I'm asking you something."

She turned her attention to him, away from the mirror. "Sure, honey," she said, with a dimpled smile. "I'll tell you. Be glad to." She looked archly and significantly into his eyes, a long, langorous look. "In the morning."

At that moment McQ was glad for all the years of training that kept his face immobile, registering neither shock, pain nor disgust. He knew what she wanted, what she was holding out for, what he had to give her, and he was glad that his face betrayed none of his distaste. He found her totally unappealing, but she said she had information, and if it led to Stan's killers, no sacrifice—and this was a whopper—would be too great.

Myra sensed his hesitation. Her face oddly childlike, she whispered to the tall detective, "You said I looked real nice. You said it. Were you lying?" there was a plea in her whispered words and italmost touched McQ.

"I never lie," he lied.

Smiling with relief and anticipation, Myra lightly touched the tip of her finegr to the line of cocaine on the glass, then slid her finger under her robe and rubbed some of the powder on her nipple. Her eyes never left McQ's, who watched in stone-faced silence, concentrating on her slender legs and the job at hand. Dipping her finger again, she slid her hand under the robe once more, lower down, reaching for the warm delta where her heavy thighs joined her belly.

He didn't flinch as she wound herself around him, her soft weight encompassing him like a hot fog, her tongue searching for his. As her hands reached for and found him, she whispered urgently in his ear, "So it's not Raquel Welch. Shut your eyes, baby, and dream."

Surprised, McQ discovered that it was going to be easier than he thought.

He hauled himself to the edge of the bed and clung there for a minute, a spent swimmer with fingers curled around a precariously floating log. Shaking his head to clear it was one of the big mistakes of his lifetime, he discovered. He glanced over his shoulder—another mistake—at Myra, who lay asleep and snoring lightly on the other half of the bed. In the harsh but true light of morning, she looked like McQ felt. He shook his head again— would he never learn?—and reached for the whiskey bottle which, with the coke and Myra's ravenous brand of kinky sex, had taken five years off his life in the last seven hours. Clutching it, he made for the bathroom.

McQ was rinsing out his mouth with rye and spitting it into the sink when he heard Myra's cooing tones through the door. They held an affection that made him wince, and the pain of the wince made him wince again.

"Lon . . . Lon, honey, you in there?"

He straightened up and hopelessly regarded his puffy face in the mirror, wishing that he were anyplace else but there. But he still had to be nice to her, long enough to collect what she owed him.

He opened the bathroom door. Myra was just slipping out of bed, pulling a robe—thank God!—over her shoulders and babbling like a newlywed.

"Look, I'll fix some eggs. You just cool it, huh? I'll make a nice pot of coffee and some toast. . . ."

McQ came in from the bathroom, busily drying his face with a towel so that he wouldn't have to look at her. "Wish I could stay, Myra, but I've got a big day," he said, forcing himself to sound affable.

The smile faded from her puppy-dog face. "Oh, sure. Well, I'm busy myself. . . ."

"Myra." Just one word, but Myra knew. Dues-paying time. It wasn't real, any of it, no matter how much she wanted to believe. It had been strictly a business deal, and she'd already had the merchandise. She took a deep breath.

"I don't know what Stan knew. I didn't tell him. I just heard it yesterday myself. Some hard rocks from out of town."

"What?" He wanted all of it. He'd given her full measure and now it was her turn. Myra nodded, understanding.

"Drug heist, like you said. They're goin' for the biggest stash in the city."

"Where?"

"You're the detective. Detect." It was a game try at independence, but it was born to lose.

"Give me some help," was all he said. But the way he said it!

"Try the place the men in blue hang out."

McQ digested this, and then realized what she was telling him. "I don't believe you," he stated flatly, his eyes slits.

Myra raised her chin in defiance. "So go find out," she challenged. "Only thing is . . . I think you better hurry."

CHAPTER VIII

The armored truck stood parked at the side entrance of the Public Safety Building, in the loading area with the ramp leading to the Police Property section. Emblazoned on its side was the seal of the State of Washington and the words "State Bureau of Narcotics." Near the truck stood a state narcotics officer in brown uniform, chatting with a headquarters man in blue. McQ had taken Myra's advice and hurried; as he rounded the corner and saw the truck, everything clicked into place and he felt very close to the answer. That is, if he were in time. The significance of the truck was not lost on him; he had to move very fast.

He strode long-legged down the headquarters lobby, past the front reception desk, as he had countless times before. But now, the uniformed officer behind the desk stopped him, challenged him politely. "Excuse me, sir, can I help you?"

With a sudden shock of mingled humiliation and pain, McQ realized that he was no longer the privileged character he used to be. In renouncing his badge and I.D., he'd given up his free access to police business and territory. But he needed an excuse to get in—desperately needed it.

"My name's McQ," he replied brusquely. "I just left the department. I want to clean out my locker."

The officer-clerk nodded. "Just a minute, sir, I'll check."

Impatient, bristling with anger and impotence, McQ stood nailed to the floor as the officer went about putting through the routine call to the personnel department, asking the expected questions and getting the expected answers. Never in his life had red tape and security been so frustrating. At last, "All right, sir," sent him loping off. But "Hold it! You'll need a visitor's pass," called him back for another bout with procedure.

Five minutes later, the demeaning visitor's pass attached to his coat, McQ made his way to the basement, where the locker room was. Looking around and finding nobody to hinder him, he walked quickly *past* the locker room and on down the hall to the police property section.

Dineen was the property officer on duty since Johnson had been murdered. He sat on a high stool behind the wire cage, locked in with several million dollars' worth of drugs, weapons and contraband, all of which represented nothing more to him than a series of file numbers. He greeted McQ cheerfully.

"Hi, Lon, what brings you around?"

"Cleaning out my locker," McQ returned easily. "How's it been?" He grinned chummily and moved closer, trying to see past Dineen's shoulder into the inner Narcotics Room.

"Oh, not bad." Ronald Dineen dearly loved to gab. "Wife's having a little problem, though. You know women. She's going into St. Joseph's tomorrow. . . ."

Meanwhile, McQ had spotted three men in the Narcotics Room. Two state narco officers were working with a headquarter's property man, unloading the room. The manila envelopes containing the drugs, almost all of it heroin and cocaine, were in the process of being removed from the room. First, the numbers were checked off on a list attached to a clipboard; then the envelopes were placed in huge plastic bags for removal. Several plastic bags, already filled with envelopes, were tied with tapes and already standing on dollies for transport out of police headquarters. The lesser materials—marijuana, kif and hashish, plus pills and syringes, spoons and cookers—were transported out in large cardboard boxes.

McQ grasped immediately what was going on. The state officers were hauling away for destruction the dangerous narcotics no longer needed as evidentiary material. Thousands of envelopes, containing a wealth of drugs whose street value was astronomical, in the millions, would be carried away and burned. McQ had seen what he'd come for. With difficulty, he tore his attention away from the narco room and back to the gynecological problems of Dineen's wife.

90

"I'm sorry about that, Ron," he said with minimal abruptness, "but it'll be okay." The two men shook hands and McQ loped out to his car.

Sitting behind the wheel of the parked TransAm, McQ surveyed the loading operation from his vantage point. The dollies of drugs were wheeled up the ramp from the property office to the loading area, where state narco officers—there were three of them all together—loaded the heavy plastic bags and cardboard boxes into the armored truck. Guarding the loading area were several uniformed city policemen, alert to danger.

Finished with the loading, one of the state officers signed the clipboard held by the property officer. Everything accounted for; nothing out of the usual. Now one of the state men climbed into the rear of the vehicle, to keep a personal eye on the goodies, while the other two got into the front seat. The truck started up and headed out of the loading area to the busy street. McQ reached down for his gun and placed it carefully on the seat beside him, tense and ready for action. He, too, pulled out of his parking space and followed the armored truck at a manageable yet discreet distance.

The truck didn't make sensational time in the heavy traffic, but it didn't seem to be in too much of a hurry. In the back, the officer sprawled at ease on the plastic bags, while up front the other two men gabbed about sports, completely relaxed. They took this trip periodically, and they knew that it was uneventful.

Only McQ was keyed up, tense, expectant. The truck could be hit at any minute, from any side. It *had* to be somewhere along here, between headquarters and the place where the drugs would be destroyed. It made sense. And McQ had to be ready for it. His hands clenched the wheel until his palms ached, and his neck craned this way and that, checking out the traffic on all sides.

Yet they went on for blocks with nothing happening. McQ's neck was beginning to ache from tension, and his shoulder muscles felt bunched. Now, suddenly, he coiled like a spring as a small van came barreling around the corner, almost hitting the state narco truck, forcing it to come to an abrupt halt. Alerted, his pulses racing, McQ hit the brakes, hard, bringing the green Pontiac to a screeching stop. He grabbed for his gun and was about to leap from the car when he saw the van driver, contrite, making his apologies to the truck and waving it on. False alarm.

McQ subsided back behind the wheel, the sudden rush of adrenalin leaving him a little spent. He watched the armored vehicle lumber on its way unruffled, and continued following in the Pontiac. Why wasn't it happening? Had Myra's information been a dud, and had the sacrifice been in vain? As they approached the outskirts of the city after an hour's uneventful driving, McQ was beginning to think so, especially when he observed that they'd reached their destination.

The vast suburban hospital complex gleamed in the bright sunshine, all efficiency and bustle. The armored truck pulled into the hospital grounds and rolled to a stop at the delivery entrance, parking next to a linen supply company truck, which stood with its back open and its ramp down as though it had just been unloaded. McQ pulled to a stop across the way, keeping his eyes peeled on the narco truck.

Coming out of the main building was a hospital security guard, uniformed and armed. The three state officers climbed from the vehicle, opened the rear doors and began to unload the plastic bags and cardboard boxes onto dollies, under the eye of the hospital guard. McQ stepped out of his car and tucked the gun inside his belt. He looked around, alert, watchful. But nothing exciting was happening.

The narcos had by now loaded the dollies; all three men wheeled them into the delivery entrance of the hospital. McQ followed inside just in time to see the dollies disappear into an elevator. One of the state men pressed a button and McQ saw the doors slide shut. Watching the indicator, he noted that the elevator was heading down for the basement and, without hesitation, he pushed through the door marked "Stairs" and took the steps down, two at a time.

The dollies arrived only seconds before he did; when he pushed open the staircase door, he saw them being wheeled down a long corridor. As he was about to follow, McQ heard a sharp and peremptory challenge.

"Hey, you, what're you doing down here?"

McQ turned to see an armed hospital security guard approaching, a scowl on his face as his fingers reached for the butt of his pistol. Thinking fast, McQ brought out the first alibi that occurred to him.

"Looking for a restroom, officer." It was a chestnut, honored by the passing of centuries, but it was undeniable and not to be questioned. A man's bladder was his private business.

"Upstairs, to the left."

"Thank you." The security guard stood his ground,

watching McQ carefully, and the tall man thought it prudent to go back through the door, upstairs and to the left.

Meanwhile, the three loaded dollies and the three state officers had reached their final destination, the furnace room deep in the hospital's belly. Lying around the room were other articles for burning, a mass of contaminated linen. One of the state officers opened the furnace door and turned to begin unloading. Suddenly, without a cry, he pitched forward on his face and fell crumpled to the floor.

The three hit men—LaSalle, Karl, and Lou from Miami—stepped out from their hiding place behind the furnace, tranquilizer guns in hand. Before the remaining two state officers could go for their weapons, the hoods had fired and all three brown-uniformed men lay sprawled face down on the furnace-room floor.

Wearing the white coveralls of linen company delivery men, the hoods worked methodically, rapidly and wordlessly, transferring the plastic bags of drugs from the dollies into three huge wheeled laundry baskets. They knew exactly what they were doing, for they ignored the cardboard boxes of marijuana entirely, taking only the heroin and the cocaine. When the bags were safely stowed, they heaped dirty sheets and towels over the tops of the baskets, concealing the priceless cargo. Then the three men wheeled the three baskets out of the laundry room and down the corridor, past the door marked "Stairs" and around the corner. The entire caper had taken less than five minutes. As they rounded the bend out of sight, the door to the stairway was pushed open and McQ came swiftly through it, having evaded the security guard. Looking around the corridor and finding it empty, he made his way to the furnace room.

One glance at the empty dollies and the sprawled bodies of the guards told him everything. For a minute he couldn't believe that the heist had actually taken place while he'd been faking a piss. With a strangled curse he ran from the room and cased the corridors again, seeing nothing but empty halls and one or two oblivious hospital personnel. He ran for the stairs, taking them three at a time all the way up.

McQ arrived at the main floor lobby just in time to see the three men wheeling the laundry carts toward the delivery entrance. The alarm bell went off in his head; he raced toward the nearest security guard.

"Call in," he shouted. "Tell them we've got a major two-eleven!"

"What?" The guard, asleep on his feet, was puzzled by the sudden appearance of this shouting wild man who towered over him.

"I'm a detective!" roared McQ. "Move it!" He gave the guard a little shove—little for McQ, but enough to rock the man off his heels—as he raced after the hit men and their cargo. But as they neared the delivery entrance, McQ forced himself to slow to a walk, so that he wouldn't blow it. He was not unaware of the possibility of being gunned down.

As they wheeled the baskets swiftly toward the hospital door, LaSalle glanced back over his shoulder and frowned deeply. He didn't like the look of the tall man behind them in the corridor; there was something about him that made the hood's hackles rise. He began to speed up slightly, and McQ walked faster to keep the pace. The carts moved even faster; so did McQ.

Suddenly, German Karl whirled and opened fire. But McQ had been anticipating the move; pulling out his own gun, he dived for cover behind a pillar as the bullets tore up the hospital corridor. Around him he could hear the screams of frightened hospital personnel who had no idea of what was taking place. Holding his arm out straight and taking steady aim, McQ squeezed off a couple of shots.

One of the gunmen, caught by McQ's slug, went down wounded; but, dragging himself up again, he ran with surprising swiftness for the truck. By now, the other two, moving very rapidly, had rushed the laundry carts up the ramp and into the truck. The driver was starting up the engine. McQ, who had been joined by a hospital guard with drawn revolver, ran the remaining few yards down the hall to the delivery entrance.

The narcotics were safe in the truck; all three hit men were inside, too. The vehicle roared away from the entrance, its back doors swinging open. As it pulled out, Lou grabbed a shotgun from the inside of the truck and opened fire through the doors, the blast slamming into the hospital entrance just as McQ and the guard emerged on the run, and driving them back momentarily.

The guard opened fire, missing the truck with every shot, but McQ, holding his fire, was racing for his car, darting through the doorway and weaving and dodging as he sprinted, to avoid bullets. Someone in the linen truck was still firing at him, the shots tearing up the lawn at his feet.

As McQ reached his car, the linen truck was moving out of the hospital grounds and off. The tall man dug out after them, barely missing an oncoming ambulance on its way in, swinging his wheel over not an instant too soon to avoid a head-on collision.

The truck sped along, gas pedal pressed to the floor, with McQ hell-for-leather after them, the souped-up engine of his Pontiac roaring through the twin exhausts. Rounding a corner with screeching tires, the linen truck beat the light and gained a momentary advantage over the Pontiac. Not that McQ would have stopped for the light, but the change brought an instant flow of cross-traffic that trapped the TransAm in its wake, leaving McQ to fume with impatience at the wheel.

Racing through traffic, the linen truck headed for the bridge, the hit men keeping an eye out for McQ. Just as they were congratulating themselves on losing him at the light, he came up, cutting in and out of traffic like a maniac, and leaving a trail of cursing drivers behind him. The bridge was up ahead.

Linking Seattle with its eastern suburbs stood the bridge, a long, modern, twin-span affair stretching its abutments out over the blue water. The top level of the bridge carried westbound traffic, into the city. The lower span carried eastbound cars, trucks and buses. As the linen truck racketed onto the westbound approach to the top level, McQ began to gain on them, pushing his customized car for all the power it could deliver.

The shotgun appeared at the open window of the truck's back door, and a hand squeezed the trigger tightly. The powerful gun let out a blast that ripped through the Pontiac's steel as McQ's car caught it broadside. The car swerved, and McQ fought a losing battle for control of the vehicle. Swerving and shimmying, bouncing out of control, the Pontiac leaped across the road divider. When McQ regained command of his car, he discovered himself on the *lower* level of the bridge, heading west while a heavy flow of bridge traffic was coming east, directly at him!

Above him, he could see the linen truck, racing across the bridge, following the normal flow of the traffic. Behind him, more traffic hemmed McQ in. Were he to get off this span and start all over again, the truck would escape for sure. There was only one thing to do, and McQ wasted no time.

Flooring the accelerator, he pushed the Pontiac forward at top speed, racing over the bridge against the flow of oncoming vehicles. The eastbound drivers could not believe their eyes. This was a nightmare, this maniac blitzkrieging them at eighty miles an hour on the wrong span! Many of the drivers simply stopped and covered their eyes until they knew that McQ was safely past them. Others roared their anger, cursing him over the blaring of their horns and his. McQ, propelled by a single purpose, halted not for man nor woman, Volkswagen or Cadillac. With his foot on the floor and his huge fist pounding the horn to clear oncoming vehicles out of his way, he barreled across, barely missing car after car, leaving the drivers shaken and white-faced.

The linen truck, having encountered no resistance, raced off the bridge at a good clip and entered the freeway. A bare minute later, McQ tore through the incredulous eastbound traffic waiting at the approach and leaped the divider again, this time on purpose, continuing his hot pursuit of the stolen drugs. Again he was gaining.

Up ahead, the linen truck, stuffed with a fortune in narcotics, screeched around a corner. Another linen-supply vehicle, identical to the first in every detail, came out of a side street to join the first one.

When McQ rounded the corner on two wheels, he couldn't believe his eyes. Through his windshield he could see, up ahead, two trucks, identical twins, racing along side by side. They were too far away for McQ to read the license plates, and he couldn't figure out which one he was after. He set his mouth in a grim smile and leaned forward, picking up more speed. Then, to his wondering eyes, appeared a *third* linen truck, the triplet, coming out of a side street to join the other two! McQ blinked in anguish as, up ahead of him, the three trucks danced a vehicular ballet, weaving in and out and around each other like the walnuts in the old shell game. Which nut held the pea? As McQ agonized, the three trucks hit a busy intersection and each roared off merrily in a different direction.

It was impossible; no way even McQ could follow three trucks at the same time, and by now he had not the smallest inkling of which of the trio held the stolen narcotics. He was outfoxed, by an operation smoother than he'd bargained for. This was no simple heist by three paid hoods; it was a tightly planned and perfectly executed maneuver in which the opposition had outclassed him all the way down the line. McQ braked furiously to a stop, and sat slamming his fists down hard on the wheel, accepting the pain gladly to take some of the bitter edge off his anger and frustration.

CHAPTER IX

Detective Burt stepped forward as Kosterman got out of his car in the headquarters' garage. Toms stood behind him, an expression of deep gloom clouding his saturnine features.

"Professional all the way," Burt informed the captain. "We found the linen truck. Switch had already been made." The three men crossed the garage to the headquarters' entrance.

"How much did they get?" demanded Kosterman.

"Property's totting it up now. Megabucks. Two million wholesale easy."

"By robbing the police. Beautiful," Toms laughed with deep bitterness. Kosterman shot him a glare of pure hatred.

"Chief wants to see you at half past," Burt told the captain. "State narco office called. Captain Windott's on his way over."

"I'll bet he is. Where's McQ?" Kosterman wanted to know.

With a jerk of his thumb, Burt indicated "upstairs." All the way up in the elevator, Toms watched the muscles of Kosterman's face drawn into a grimace of loathing and frustration. But the captain didn't utter a syllable until he flung open the door of his office. Then he erupted.

"What the hell was that? Just what in hell was that, hot-dogging it around like that?" His voice was strangled with rage.

McQ turned from the window, taking in the livid Kosterman, the silent Toms and the eager Burt, who was already on the phone, giving orders. "I'll need about twenty-five. Now. No, I'll need another detail for that. . . ."

"I wasn't sure of my information," drawled McQ. "By the time it proved out. . . ."

"You didn't have to be sure!" screamed Kosterman. "Your responsibility was to let us know!"

McQ's back stiffened. "My responsibility," he advised Kosterman crisply, sure of his ground, "was to my client. Nothing in the law says I had to tell you anything."

Kosterman's sullen silence was a tacit acknowledgement of the truth of this. Still, the captain had clout and he intended to use it on McQ, as long and as hard as it would carry.

"Okay." Kosterman drew a deep breath. "Then you better tell 'your client' to get himself a new private. Pending a look into that shootout, there'll be a delay in approving Pinky's request to take you on."

This could be a serious setback, not being licensed immediately through Pinky. But McQ's craggy face revealed its usual zilch. Burt, finishing his phone conversation, cut in, addressing the captain.

"Okay. We're set. I'll handle the sweep on Santiago's plant. Ernie'll handle his house. Ed . . . even if Santiago's got it, it won't be stashed there."

Kosterman nodded agreement. "I know. Play it out." Eager to get started, Burt took his bright eyes and bushy tail out the door.

Toms turned to Kosterman, speaking seriously, the note of bitter levity gone. "Ed, help me with something here. Let's assume for the moment that McQ is right. Santiago needed the dope to supply his people, so he brought in the robbery team. But how did he know *when* it was going to be moved? How did he know *where* it was going to be burned? I understand that's secret information."

"Yes. State picks time and place."

"Then somebody leaked it," concluded Toms.

"Somebody," agreed Kosterman. There was a pause as this fact sunk in on all of them. This was indeed an added complication to a bitch of a case. A man on the inside!

"What about a connection between the robbery and the murders of Boyle and the officers?"

"They connect all right," McQ put in. "One of the officers killed worked the property department: Wally Johnson."

Resenting his interference, Kosterman glared murder at the tall man. Then he turned to the mayor's liaison. "We're aware of that, Frank. If there's a tie-in, we'll find it." Turning back to McQ, the captain snarled, "You forget something. You're out!"

With a grin, McQ headed for the exit. "You know what? I like it."

"Just a minute," Kosterman barked after him. "You still carrying?"

McQ hesitated for the merest fraction of a second, but it was long enough to tell Kosterman "yes."

"Better leave it," the captain ordered. "For the time being your permit's revoked." It was more clout and it felt good to Kosterman.

McQ just looked at him; not a muscle twitched in his rugged face. Unperturbed, he hauled the revolver out of his belt and laid it down on Kosterman's desk.

"Now out!" Kosterman felt power swelling all through him. He'd expected an argument, but McQ hadn't delivered it. "If I get any more crap from you you'll find employment of any kind a little out of your reach. And if you want me to hit you harder I'll do that too." Kosterman had never dreamed that this moment would come, giving him complete mastery over McQ, and he reveled in it, gloating.

McQ, showing no emotion, turned to go as the intercom buzzer sounded. Kosterman clicked it on.

"Captain Windott's here, sir," the metallic voice squawked through the machine.

"Fine. Send him in." Kosterman was set up to deal with anything or anybody now. As McQ opened the door to leave, Windott, his stern face grimly set, brushed past him. Windott and McQ exchanged long, serious glances. Then Kosterman moved forward to make introductions.

"Bill, you know Frank Toms from the mayor's office. Captain Windott, State Narcotics. . . ." As he ushered Windott in, Kosterman's hand shot out and closed the door on McQ, shutting him completely out of police business.

The officer on duty at the police property office today was Paul Czernik; he sat perched at his post, on the high stool behind the wire partition. McQ breezed in with a big smile, rapping.

"Paul, Mrs. Johnson says Wally left some family pictures back in the lounge. Could you get them, please?"

The property officer looked at McQ, puzzled. Surely McQ no longer belonged here. McQ caught the vibes and decided to brazen it out. In for a sheep.

"Didn't you hear? I'm back on." He jerked his head in the direction of the electronically controlled door to the property room. "Give me some juice, will you? I want to use the phone."

Convinced, Czernik flashed McQ a wide smile. "Hey, that's terrific!" he congratulated as he pressed the buzzer, admitting Lon.

McQ strolled in and headed for the phone. Picking up the receiver, he prompted Paul, "Wally and his wife at the beach. Something like that."

"I'll see what I can find," the officer promised, going off.

McQ, holding the phone, followed Paul with his eyes until the officer disappeared into the lounge. Then he put down the phone, leaving it off the hook so it wouldn't ring, and took a good look around. The coast was clear. He walked swiftly to the room where the guns were stored, rows and rows of confiscated weapons. Most of them had been used in

crimes and each was tagged with identifying information and docket number. Over one group of guns
was a sign reading "No Longer Needed as Evidentiary Material," and it was to these weapons that
McQ headed like a homing pigeon.

He checked out the room. Way in back, another
property officer worked at tagging bicycles; he had
no interest in observing McQ. Satisfied, the tall man
quickly but carefully selected a snub-nosed .38,
shoving it into his belt. Now his eye fell on something
that kindled his immediate interest; it appeared to be
a gun shoulder stock. He took it quietly from the
rack and slipped it under his jacket, and again
checked out the room. He could see Czernik approaching at a distance. McQ moved quickly; he was
just putting the telephone receiver back in its cradle
when the property officer came up.

"Nothing back there, Lon. Are you sure?"

McQ shrugged. "She's probably mistaken," he
drawled. "Thanks anyway." He didn't wave, but
kept his arms close at his side as he was buzzed out
of the electronic door, holding the stolen stock close
against his body. He had what he'd come for; McQ
was armed and ready to roll once more.

McQ rummaged busily in the trunk of his car,
moving large objects to the sides and piling clothes
on top of them until he had cleared a space in the
center. Reaching in, he lifted out a section of the
trunk flooring, exposing a hidden compartment.
From under his coat he took the pilfered gun stock
and laid it carefully in the compartment, checking
to see that it fit and wasn't crammed in. Then he
replaced the flooring and slammed the trunk shut. As

he moved around to the driver's door, he looked from the window of the second level of the parking garage to the street below.

Kosterman, Toms, Chief Grogan, and Captain Windott came out of the Public Safety Building, walking with purposeful strides, like a small army. McQ watched them from above as they walked down the street one block, to City Hall. He saw them enter the tower building and realized that they were about to attend a top-level conference. Rubbing his chin for a beat, McQ stood thinking, putting it together in his head. Then he climbed into the Pontiac and drove down the ramp to the street.

It was not a romantic restaurant, more of a business place, actually, a downtown restaurant near the complex of municipal buildings and the Civic Center. It was frequented by politicians, lawyers and upper-echelon personnel from the government buildings, who seemed to prefer the heavy, wood-paneled walls to soft lights and music. It was a place that had a solid feel to it, and McQ liked it because it was nice and not posh, and because he felt comfortable there. And he felt comfortable with Lois, too, anywhere at all.

He and Lois picked at the food on their plates as Frank Toms sipped at his drink. He'd bumped into them having dinner, and joined them, although he'd been waiting for some people. They had kept the conversation strictly personal, with no references to the heist.

"I can get you some clerical work in Accounting if you like, Lois," Toms was saying. "If you're willing to wait, something more interesting might open in Public Affairs."

"Thank you, Frank," Lois smiled at him sweetly. "Let me think about it."

"Certainly, no rush." Toms turned to McQ. "Lon, can I talk to you for a minute?"

McQ rose instantly and followed Toms to the bar, where the two men stood talking quietly together.

"I agree with you," said Toms. "I think the murders are locked in with the robbery somehow. At first I didn't. I thought Ed had the right handle on it. But now I think there's a lot more to this than it seemed. With the mayor's permission, I intend to take it up with the commission."

"Thanks for telling me," said McQ.

"But if I were you," warned Toms, "I'd watch myself. I think you're very exposed. Excuse me, now. There's my party."

McQ looked after Toms as he went to join another man and two women. He walked slowly back to Lois, who scanned the frown on his face. She put down her knife and fork, wondering.

"Problem?"

"No. Go on, eat up." He sat down heavily at the table, abstracted, as Lois went back to her food.

When he took her home, Lois invited him in for a nightcap and McQ accepted. Throwing the lock on his car, he escorted her into the building, admiring her slender figure from behind and the graceful yet unaffected way she carried herself.

The apartment was pleasant; McQ had always felt at home there. Nothing grand, it reflected a modest income combined with good taste. There were quite a few house plants around; Lois had a green thumb. She chatted to him as she mixed two highballs.

"I *am* gong down to see my folks. Why don't you drive me? What else have you got to do?"

"Like to, but not right now," was McQ's only reply, but Lois took it to mean that he was still on the case.

"I see," she said stiffly. Then, with more warmth, "Lon, why don't you catch on? Police work . . . it can't be done. Not these days. It's bailing out a tidal wave with a paper cup. Crime isn't just organized, it's institutionalized!"

McQ had to smile at the fierce expression on her ordinarily gentle face. He took the drink from her hand; his only reply to her angry words was "Thanks."

"You know," she continued, "I've been wondering what you'd do if it wasn't Stan who was killed. If it was a new partner, someone you didn't even like." She shook her dark head; the hair swirled out like a dusky cloud across the nape of her slim neck. "I know," she sighed in resignation, "the same thing. You can't help yourself. You're programmed. I saw it in Stan. You become a cop, it's more exciting than pumping gas; a man can be a man, he thinks. Pretty soon you're handcuffed to it. It's taking you; you lose charge. Well, you're blowing it, you know."

"What?"

"Your allotment, brother." Bitterness crept into Lois's voice. "Tick, tick, tick, tick. . . . You're off the force, you won't get licensed. You're no kid and you're empty. Why don't you find something filling?"

"Don't you want to know who killed Stan?" He

hurled the question at her harder than he'd intended. "Don't you want to know why?"

"Yes, you'd think I would, wouldn't you?" She hurled her words right back at him. "Well, anesthesia has set in. Santiago did it; Santiago didn't do it; what's the difference? You know what I really want?"

"What?" He did want to know.

"Amnesia." She uttered a short, humorless laugh.

The ringing of the telephone surprised them both, so wrapped up in their argument were they, so very close to communicating. Lois merely looked at the phone for four rings, then she picked it up.

"Hello. . . . Yes, he's still here." She handed McQ the phone without another word.

"Yeah," he barked into the receiver.

J.C. was calling him from a pay phone near Santiago's meat-packing plant. Behind him, the police search team was leaving, climbing into their cars in pairs and going off.

"Lon, search is over," J.C. reported.

"What did they find?"

"What we figured. Zip."

"Okay. Thanks. Go home." McQ hung up the phone and squared his wide shoulders. "Nothing," he said in answer to the unspoken question on Lois's face.

"Then Santiago doesn't have it."

"He has it." McQ spoke with harsh bitterness born of frustration. "Driving it around the city, probably. That's standard. Now what's a good safe place to stash it, would you say?"

Lois thought for a minute, her lovely brow wrinkling in concentration. "Where the police have already been," she decided.

110

"I think so too."

"Are you leaving?"

"No big hurry," said McQ.

"Refill?"

"No, thanks, I'm fine."

Lois paused. There was evidently something heavy on her mind, judging from the expression on her face. Then she apparently made up her mind, for she placed a soft hand on McQ's sleeve and looked up into his rough-hewn face, her eyes meeting his.

"Lon . . . can I tell you something?"

"Sure."

"Stan and I were having trouble. For a long time. We were in the same bed, but it was for sleeping." Lois searched McQ's face for a reaction. "Didn't he say anything? Didn't he tell you I was leaving him?" She pressed for an answer.

McQ answered truthfully. "No."

Lois pushed a strand of hair off her forehead, smiling wryly. "And I thought partners know everything about each other."

"Everything and nothing," said McQ.

Lois lifted her blue eyes to his again. Her long black lashes were wet with unshed tears, and her mouth trembled with a suppressed sensuality that caught at his throat. "Lon." Her voice was barely above a whisper, resonant with huskiness. "I don't want you for a brother. I haven't for some time now."

This was the very first time that Lois Boyle had come on to him, the first time that words like these had passed her lips. But McQ knew that it had always been there between them; it went way, way back. Even when Stan had been alive. Saying nothing, he looked down at the play of emotion over her beautiful face, and tried to sort out his feelings.

"That's the danger of the buddy system," Lois laughed. "Maybe the manual needs rewriting." She tilted her head to smile wryly up at him.

"Maybe." He returned the wry smile.

"Well, why not, Lon?" Her voice was as soft and promising as a feather bed. "A couple of empties. You know, like in the songs. Let's help each other through the night."

Now she was standing so close to him that he could smell the jasmine scent she wore. Tempted, he looked down at her. A lovely woman full of untapped feelings, she was like a gift from the gods. It would be so nice; why was he hesitating?

She closed her eyes and shivered a little, waiting for his touch. Very, very gently, he put his hand on her face. She tilted it up like a flower as he caught her in his arms and kissed her mouth. Her passionate arms pulled his hard-muscled body closer to her softness, and her lips responded to his as though starving for his kiss.

The burglar alarm on McQ's Pontiac went off with a shrill scream, disrupting the kiss and breaking the mood. What a hell of a time for the "attractive nuisance" to call for attention! Irritated, McQ released Lois and headed for the front door to investigate. She laughed shakily, and smoothed her rumpled hair and dress.

Although the alarm was cutting the air into ribbons, there was no thief in sight, only a few civilians, drawn by the sound and expecting action. Annoyed, McQ turned off the siren, then looked up at Lois's window. Her slim body was silhouetted against the glass as she stood looking down at him, waiting for him to come back and take her to bed.

But McQ was in the chill night air now, his romantic mood changed to one of action. The case was pressing on him, driving him to move, to get going. He looked up at Lois once again, then decided. Climbing into the Pontiac, he drove off.

Lois stood watching from the window for a minute or two after McQ's car turned the corner. Then she turned away.

CHAPTER X

He opened the trunk and rummaged through it in the darkness, his eyes accustomed to working at night. Moving the stuff around in the trunk, McQ fished out a toolbox and opened it. He took from it a flashlight, a set of lock picks and an Ace lock-picking tool. This last item resembled a small screwdriver handle with metal prongs, and was used to turn the barrel locks on burglar alarms. Stowing these articles in his pocket, McQ prepared himself fully for a professional burglary operation.

He bent to open the compartment in the trunk floor, and tenderly lifted out the gun stock he'd filched from the property section. Standing, he opened up the stock. Nestled inside the stock was a broomstick Mauser 7.63 automatic pistol, a monster weapon holding many cartridges. With the stock attached the Mauser could be used as a rifle; alone it made a dandy pistol. It all fitted neatly together, appearing, when folded up, as an innocuous shoulder stock, useful but hardly deadly. But it was deadly. He patted the 7.63 fondly, then dived down again for a handful of ammo, with which he loaded the automatic pistol. Then, carrying the Mauser without the stock attachment, he locked the trunk and came out of the alley where he'd parked.

The Santiago Meat Packing Company was closed for the night; the complex was deserted and McQ muffled his footsteps as he crossed the dark, empty street. A watchman was making his rounds, checking windows, doors and gates; he was an armed and uniformed private security guard. McQ scrunched up against the heavy chain-link fence, waiting immobile until the guard had passed. Then his long legs took the fence easily, in a single catlike bound.

Moving silently inside the complex, McQ crossed an open area, heading for a metal stairway that went up the outside of the main plant building. Up the stairs to a side door; he found it locked, just as he'd expected. He cast his eye over the dark complex below, constantly aware of the possibility of the guard's reappearance. Then he turned his attention to the door.

His first obstacle was defeating the alarm system. Taking the Ace lock-picking tool from his pocket, he found the alarm cylinder implanted in the door and gently began to ease the prongs of the tool into it. Great care and expertise were required; the alarm was delicate and one half of a false move would set the whole thing off, as intended. Gingerly, McQ worked the prongs, not hurrying, bending all his attention on the fragile junction between cylinder and pick. Then, after two long minutes of barely breathing, a quick snap of his powerful wrist turned the lock, effectively shutting off the alarm system.

McQ stood erect to fill his lungs with air; although the night was chilly, he was sweating visibly. Looking out again for the guard, his glance swept the ground below. All quiet. Now for the next hurdle: to effect entry. He took out his lock picks and got to work on the door.

The guard was inside, making his rounds in the shipping section. Throwing the beam of his flashlight around, he shone it on the very door on which McQ, outside, was picking the lock. Neither man was aware of the other, and the door inside was intact as far as the guard could see. He moved along to another section of the building.

Only seconds later, the metal clamp which effected the electrical connection from the door to the door frame popped open and McQ slipped silently into the plant. Shutting the door behind him, he reset the metal clamp, just in case the guard should come through, checking again. Then he turned around to get his bearings, his eyes straining in the interior blackness.

He was in the shipping section, a very large room with large crates of meat stacked high, waiting to be shipped out. Around the walls stood dollies and handtrucks for moving the boxes. Racks were attached to the ceiling; from some of them sausages and frankfurters were dangling in chains. Others held heavy, streaky slabs of bacon. Tubs of sausage meat stood heaped high. The room was heavily refrigerated, and McQ hunched up a bit against the cold, moving deeper into the section to begin his search, Mauser ready at his side.

In the semi-darkness and deep shadows, he moved without a sound through the various sections of the meat-packing plant, past the huge processing machines that turned great carcasses into supermarket cuts, past the conveyer belts, the racks and giant hooks, the tubs for scraps and suet, the long, thin knives attached by magnets to the stainless steel working surfaces. Everywhere he went McQ felt the chill deepen around him, cutting him to the bone and penetrating his liver and kidneys.

Here and there, night lights were on, casting long, ominous shadows over the strange shapes of the equipment. McQ used his flashlight sparingly, merely clicking it on and off as he made his examination from room to room. Through the entire plant he went: the sausage-making room, the boning room, the smoke houses, the hog-cutting room, each a marvel of cleanliness and efficiency. But his search seemed hopeless. There was nothing.

Every now and then McQ would encounter the security guard on his perpetual rounds. Ducking into a shadow, the tall man watched the watchman who watched the plant. Then, keeping his eye peeled on the guard's movements, McQ would move silently off in the opposite direction or slip unnoticed up a stairway.

By now McQ had reached the warehouse section of the plant. He moved through it, searching quickly, yet missing nothing of importance. It seemed hopeless, and the tall man began to admit to himself his disappointment. Yet he kept on going . . . through the warehouse . . . past a storage room . . . past a laboratory, locked, but with a window into which he peered. Nothing. Nothing.

He was about ready to give up. But as he turned the corner, McQ clicked his light on and the beam fell on a door with sign reading "Spice Room. Authorized Personnel Only." Clicking off the light, he turned the doorknob carefully, silently, and entered.

He again switched on the light beam, casting it around the room. Spices and condiments of every description stood in hundred-pound barrels and large bins all around the room. And then the flashlight picked up the dull gleam of plastic. There they were, the plastic bags stolen from the state narcotics officers! A few of the bags were still full, but most were empty, and the manila envelopes that held the drugs were strewn all around the room.

He'd found it. He was right and the rest of them had been wrong. Spotting a wall phone, McQ stepped to it and took it off the hook to see whether there was a night connection to an outside line. The sudden pressure of metal on the back of his head made him freeze. A long-barreled automatic, silencer attached, was pressed up against the base of his skull.

"Easy. Let it slide to the floor," the man's voice said.

McQ dropped the Mauser gently, as ordered. The lights went on, revealing one of Santiago's men holding the gun on McQ, while Santiago himself stood in the doorway, one hand on the light switch. He entered the room, followed by two more hoods.

Santiago's face showed the aftereffects of the beating he'd received from the hands of McQ. His nose, reset, was bandaged heavily, and there were the marks of stitches over his left cheekbone and right eye. The eye itself was puffed out to twice its normal size. The hoods spread themselves around the room while the gunman, without removing the barrel from McQ's skull, stooped quickly to pick up the Mauser and tossed it aside.

Surrounded, Lon McQ knew that he was in deep trouble. Even though only the first man held a gun, McQ was positive that all the others were well armed.

"Department knows I'm here," he said conversationally to Santiago. "I've got a back-up unit in case I'm not out in five more minutes."

But the other was not so easily bluffed. "No, you are alone," he retorted. "You have been observed from the roof." Unhurriedly, Santiago moved to the table on which sat a number of manila narcotics' envelopes, some coffee cups and a pot of coffee, still hot. He sat down, regarding McQ with something very similar to amusement.

"Breaking and entering. Very serious," he smiled.

"Robbery. Possession of narcotics. Your trouble is bigger than mine," retorted McQ, in a magnificent disregard of the situation.

"Well," said Santiago, "we shall see." He held his hand up to his face. "Look," he ordered. "I do not like what you did to me. Still, I understand. I suppose I do. The rage of a man who has lost a good friend. But I do not like what you did."

"Too bad," shrugged McQ. "I enjoyed it myself." His cool seemed to astound Santiago, who looked at him blankly for an instant, then smiled.

"You have interrupted my coffee." He turned to one of his men. "Pour a cup for Mr. McQ."

"No, never mind," said McQ. But it was too late. Santiago's hood had already begun pouring coffee into the second cup.

"Oh, come on now, relax," Santiago urged with urbane charm. He smiled again, obviously in no hurry to finish his game with McQ. It was cat and mouse, but McQ couldn't quite figure it.

"One spoonful or two?" asked Santiago. Then he answered his own question. "Two. It has been my observation that policemen like their coffee sweet."

And then Santiago did a very strange thing. Picking a knife up from the table, he jabbed it into one of the manila narcotics envelopes and ripped it open. Then he took a spoon, dipped it into the white substance in the torn envelope and put two spoonfuls into one of the coffee cups.

McQ watched him closely, eyes narrowed, not yet guessing Santiago's game. He saw the Spaniard take another spoonful out of the envelope, put it into his own cup, stir it and drink.

Now McQ was beginning to see light at the end of the tunnel. He walked across to the table, picked up the slashed envelope and tasted its contents. Nodding to himself in confirmation of his hunch, McQ picked up two more envelopes at random and ripped them open, tasting the white powder. The same as the first. He cocked his head at Santiago.

"Sugar," the Spaniard said. Then rage seized him. "All of them! Sugar, sugar, sugar!" He swept the envelopes off the table with a contemptuous gesture of his manicured hand. Now he was screaming. "We have stolen sugar! Do you understand? THE DRUGS HAVE BEEN REMOVED! A SWITCH HAS

TAKEN PLACE! AND WHERE? WHERE ELSE? *IN THE POLICE DEPARTMENT ITSELF!*

As this new information sank in, McQ's face for the first time betrayed the impact the knowledge had on him. Santiago gulped for air, making a tremendous effort to regain control over himself, and slowly calming down. When he had attained mastery over his emotions, he ventured another smile.

"Well, I think it is charming. I arrange a robbery. A *difficult* robbery, stealing from the police itself. So *they* steal from me before I can steal from them. I find it very embarrassing. Proof once again. It is unfair." He gave a Latin shrug. "The advantage lies with the people on the inside."

McQ wasn't finding any of this funny. "Who?" he demanded.

Santiago spread out his hands, palms upward, in an age-old gesture of ignorance. "How would I know? I am on the outside. Big people, it would seem. Big operation, who else but big people?"

McQ added this to the data file in his head. One irony did strike him, peculiar to this situation. Here they were, a hood and a busted cop, trying to figure out which of the police were crooked.

"What about Stan? Did you off him?"

"No. Look inside also. Possibly he discovered what was taking place. Possibly it has been going on for some time. Possibly all that *ever* got burned in our city was sugar. I find that fascinating. Certain officials are my competitors. Business does take strange turns." He shook his head in admiration of the complexities of life.

McQ said, "I'm going."

"Go. I have nothing to fear from you." Santiago

waved his hand at the envelopes. "All this will be destroyed. No one will know a thing about . . . my embarrassment. Except those very clever people on the inside who will know it all." He sighed in exquisite resignation.

"My gun," said McQ, holding out his hand.

"Certainly," Santiago was all old-world courtesy. He gestured to his man to fetch McQ's Mauser. "Oh, yes," he added, "but first there is one thing more." Catching McQ unaware, Santiago drove his heavily muscled forearm into McQ's middle, doubling him over from the force of the blow.

Moving in to help, Santiago's hoods were waved off by their boss. This was something he'd been saving for himself, some small compensation for his loss of face . . . twice. He kicked savagely at McQ's head and kidneys, thrilling to the impact of his shoe on the taller man's flesh. As McQ attempted to rise to his feet, Santiago lashed out again and again, cruel blows that found their target. He battered McQ without mercy until the big man slumped unconscious, then he kicked him twice more, as interest on the repayment of the beating McQ had given him. The last thing McQ heard before he blacked out was the sound of gloating laughter.

He regained partial consciousness, only to be overwhelmed by fresh waves of pain that coursed through his body when Santiago's men dumped him brutally on the ground near his car. McQ lay without moving on the chilly earth, not daring to move, hardly believing that he was still alive. Hearing a click close to his head, the big man made a gargantuan effort and rolled over on his back, his face all bloody, staring up into the blackness.

He was surrounded by Santiago's hoods, one of whom had the Mauser pointed down at McQ. It was the hammer he'd heard click. Unable to move, McQ stared into the barrel of the gun. The hood pulled the trigger. Click. Click. Click. The gun was empty, evidently an uproarious joke, for all of the men were laughing. Except McQ, who tried to struggle up on one elbow. In contempt, the hood tossed the Mauser to the ground, following it with the scattered handful of bullets. Then the hoods turned and walked off, leaving McQ to sink back on the ground as the blackness again washed over him.

CHAPTER XI

Pinky Farrow pressed the wet towel to McQ's battered face, gently wiping away the blood and filth and trying to bring down the swelling. McQ lay stretched out, bare-chested, on the couch in his messy apartment, suffering under Pinky's ministrations, every inch of his face and body an ache or a pain. Finally, he'd had enough, and pushed Pinky's hands away, muttering "Okay."

He stood unsteadily and walked across to the mirror, where he studied his pulped face, wincing.

"Not too bad," Farrow called out encouragingly. "Just looks like you're wearing a fright mask."

McQ turned away from the mirror. "Pinky, I'd like to buy you," he said through puffed and broken lips.

The older man frowned helplessly. "Lon, it's a high-level rip-off. Right in keeping with the custom of the day. I can't be much help on it."

"I think you can," returned McQ. "I'll pay you whatever you like."

Pinky waved a protesting hand. "Not the money . . . I don't want to mix it with the tall fellows. Ruffle the wrong feathers and my door gets shut and bolted. Go to Internal Affairs. It's their kind of work," he advised.

McQ barked a short, scornful laugh. "Who watches the cops who watch the cops? It's okay, Pinky, I understand." He patted the old detective sympathetically as he turned away to button on his shirt.

Pinky felt lousy, as though he were letting McQ down. "What would you want from me?" he asked reluctantly.

McQ's swollen face broke into a painful smile. "Your time, your head. You wouldn't have to do anything you didn't want."

Pinky thought for a minute, sighing. Then he relented. "Okay. On one condition."

"What?"

"It's for free."

McQ smiled again, then he was all serious business. "Okay. Let's see what we can put together. Two separate frolics here. Santiago arranged the heist and came up a loser. Somebody, *somebodies* on the inside lifted the dope first. Wally Johnson was on the morning watch, alone. Easy for him to have slipped out the junk and slipped in the sugar. His murder, Hyatt's and Stan's connect with the dope

switch. They have nothing to do with militants."
McQ concluded his recital of relevant data.

"Makes you wonder, doesn't it," asked Pinky,
"why Kosterman pressed so hard to stick them?"

"Yeah, doesn't it?" McQ agreed. "You get on
Wally Johnson's wife. Get a line on his friends, see
who you can tie him in with. Hyatt, too."

"What are you going to do?" Pinky asked.

"Get inside . . . on Kosterman."

Pinky just looked at his partner. That was heavy.

"Now, look," McQ continued. "By now the dope's
been collected and stashed someplace—"

"Unless it's already on the streets," Pinky interrupted.

"Let's find out," said McQ. He picked up the
phone and dialed police headquarters. "Sergeant
Davis," he told the operator.

J. C. answered the phone. "Sergeant Davis."

"J. C. . . . Lon. I need something. Can you talk?
Has a new supply of junk hit the street?"

"No, not a thing."

"Okay, if it does, let me know."

"Sure," agreed J.C. "What is this? What are you
into?"

"Don't ask. Just answer. It's better that way. Talk
to you." McQ hung up, leaving a puzzled J.C. to
think briefly. The young black detective turned to
Kosterman.

"McQ," he told him, watching Kosterman's face
go hard.

McQ drove the Pontiac into the lot from headquarters and got out. He stood looking across at the
large building, men and women moving in and out

of the doors in a steady stream. It was in there, it was all in there, the answer to everything. Crossing the lot, he made his way to the building and on into the lobby.

A small clubby group of brass stood at the little cigar store in the main corridor, talking and buying. McQ spotted Kosterman, Chief Grogan and a couple of other officials. The little group exuded a tight-knit, "in" vibration. McQ watched as Kosterman bought a cigar, and the little group divided to go separate ways. The tall man moved quickly to catch up with the police captain.

"Ed, can I talk to you?" asked McQ.

Kosterman merely looked at him and kept moving, peeling the cellophane off the cigar tube and taking the cigar out as he walked. He said nothing. McQ moved along at his side; they were walking in the direction of the security desk that guarded the entrance into headquarters proper. McQ arranged his bruised features in an expression of contrition, and was careful to keep it there as he talked.

"Ed, I've been doing a lot of thinking. I was wrong. Stubborn, uncooperative. . . . I'd like back in."

Kosterman stopped, but it was only to throw the cigar wrappings in the trash can. He hardly seemed interested in anything McQ had to say. They had reached the security desk, and the captain turned to McQ.

"File your application with the commission. You have a right."

"It'll come back to you, anyway. I could use a supportive letter," McQ wheedled.

But his plea elicited no response from Kosterman, who was lavishing all his attention on his cigar.

Now McQ appeared at his most contrite. "Ed, I'm eating it. I'll be a good boy."

Abruptly, Kosterman bit off the end of his cigar. "I'll think about it," was the only crumb he threw to McQ as he crossed past the security guard to the bank of elevators, into territory forbidden to McQ, who stood in the lobby watching him go.

Frank Toms accompanied the mayor and his aide out of City Hall and walked with them over to the mayor's designated limousine, sitting at the curb, chauffeur waiting. The mayor and the aide climbed into the back seat, and Toms stuck his head in the car window for a final word with His Honor. As the limousine pulled away from the curb and he started to walk up the street, Toms was somewhat startled to be met by McQ, who had obviously been waiting for him.

"Frank. . . ."

Toms stared at him. He'd never seen McQ in this condition before.

"I need your clout," the big man pleaded. "Don't ask me why. Just do it for me."

"If I can," Toms said in a rather reserved manner.

"I want back with the department," explained McQ. "I talked with Ed. He just said he'd think about it."

"Be glad to do what I can. . . . Do you know what you're doing?"

With a small smile, McQ replied, "Well, I'll soon find out, won't I?"

The glittering surface of the glass high-rise reflected the sun and the towers of business and industry that surrounded it. The elevator carried McQ up in carpeted comfort to one of the highest floors, Muzak singing to him for the duration of the climb. As McQ stepped off the elevator, he bore left and pushed his way through a pair of elegant glass and walnut doors with the firm's name etched in gold leaf. A switchboard operator-receptionist was trilling into her headpiece.

"Lowell, Fitzpatrick, attorneys at law. No, sir, Mr. Lowell is in a meeting. May I have him return the call? Certainly, Senator, as soon as possible." She motioned McQ to a deep settee when he stated his business, and he settled into its elegant comfort. But he didn't have long to wait. Andrew Lowell walked out of the meeting when he heard that McQ was calling on him, and ushered him courteously into his own private office.

It was a room bespeaking both money and taste. Very expensively furnished in modern woods, chrome and glass, with one or two large contemporary paintings that McQ instinctively knew must have cost a king's ransom apiece, even though he himself preferred to look anywhere but at them. But then, McQ only knew what he liked. Andrew Lowell, a senior partner in the high-powered, very much in demand law firm, was expensively furnished himself. His five-hundred-dollar suit reeked of conservatism and he waved McQ to a Mies van der Rohe leather and steel chair.

"Lon, nice to see you. It's been some time." He didn't mention McQ's welts and bruises, being too much of a gentleman.

"Andrew," acknowledged the big man, shaking hands.

They sat side by side in the fine grained leather

chair, a small coffee table of glass and metal between them.

"May I get something? Coffee? A drink?" Lowell offered.

"No, thanks." McQ shook his head. His eyes widened as he took notice of the exquisite model of a large yacht sitting on a table against the wall. Lowell followed his glance.

"Nice, isn't it? The office is having it made. Some of our people like to talk in the fresh air." He paused, then began again. "I hear you're having a little trouble. I'm sorry about that."

"Happens."

Lowell understood that McQ's visit wasn't frivolous, but he was a patient man—one had to be in the legal profession, where important matters can take as long as decades to untangle—and he was willing to make frivolous conversation.

"I know," he said, "you want us to sue the police department for some fancy figures."

McQ smiled back. "With your style, they wouldn't have a chance." Now he went to work in earnest, as smooth as silk, putting on the pressure with the lightest of touches. "Andrew, funny, but I suddenly got to wondering about the Van Cortland boy."

"Doing fine," replied Lowell. "Very valuable lesson he learned about possession. His parents still say how appreciative they are of the quiet way you got the D.A. to reject the complaint."

"Glad to have been of help. I was wondering too about that client of yours from up north. Remember, the one who got mixed up with that bimbo who had a field day with his credit cards?"

"Brewster," supplied the lawyer. "He's very appreciative, too. *And* a lot more careful now about where he takes off his trousers." Lowell smiled, well aware of what McQ was up to, but he enjoyed watching the big man operate.

"That's good," said McQ.

"What is this, Lon? A stroll through memory lane . . . or collection time?"

"You have it, Andrew," conceded McQ. "I was thinking too about that little problem you had. . . ."

Lowell was not embarrassed that easily. "Yes," he acknowledged, "I'm very appreciative too . . . and very careful about mixing drinking and driving. Lon, you're dropping mother bombs. It's not necessary, you know. We're very good at repaying debts."

McQ was not embarrassed easily, either. "Only to show you the kind of thing this is. I can't take a 'no' from you."

"What do you need?" Lowell came directly to the point.

"IRS stuff. Income tax returns that maybe show some unusual intake. Maybe a Swiss bank account . . . or a hidden safe-deposit box."

"From whom?"

"Ed Kosterman, Captain."

Lowell said nothing for a few moments. He hadn't expected anything that heavy. This was indeed collection time. At last he said crisply, "I see. Don't tell me why."

"I wasn't going to, but there's some hurry on it. Take a lot of chasing for me to track it down. I thought I'd rush it along by coming to where the tentacles start."

"How can I reach you?" asked Lowell. McQ handed him a slip of paper.

131

"Here's a phone number. Just leave a message, hit or miss. I'll get back to you."

"Fine." Lowell rose from his chair. Now that business had been concluded, all was pleasant once more. "Nice seeing you, Lon. Don't stay away so long. Let's do lunch at my club."

"Sure," said McQ. "I'd like that." He knew it would never happen. But he hoped he'd get what he'd come there for. Asking hadn't been easy.

CHAPTER XII

McQ and Pinky Farrow walked along the path in Kinnear Park. It was a beautiful day, the kind that brought out young lovers to stroll and frail old ladies to sun themselves on the benches. Kids played on the grass, tossing frisbees and balls back and forth, and young mothers pushed strollers and carriages.

"Hyatt had been walking the streets for thirty years," Pinky was saying. "I don't think he ever fired a shot in the line of duty."

"How was he fixed?" asked McQ.

"Four sons in the construction business. Gave him everything. Stayed on as a patrolman because he liked it."

Perplexity wrinkled McQ's forehead. None of this made any sense, yet it had to be connected somewhere. "Doesn't figure. He and Wally Johnson were taken off with the same gun. It has to connect."

"I know, but I'm telling you. He just doesn't figure in a frolic."

"What did you get from Wally Johnson's wife?"

"Nothing. She's left the city, destination as yet unknown."

McQ tried to code this information into the data file he kept in his head, but he could get no connections. Nothing seemed to figure. He nibbled at his upper lip in frustration, uncertain what to do next. "Okay, keep after it," he told Pinky.

The older man stopped on the path. "Lon, we're having a little family thing Sunday. Nothing special. Barbecue, some chickens or something. My kids'll be over, grandkids. Like to have you join us." It was a sincere offer, sincerely made, and McQ was both touched and pleased.

But "Thanks, Pinky, but I don't want to make any plans now." He patted the older man on the shoulder and walked off without another word. Farrow stood looking after his tall frame with sympathy. McQ was really a loner; Pinky, surrounded by a large family, felt a pang of pity for the younger man.

Myra paused in the doorway of the coffee shop, scanning the faces. It didn't take her long to find McQ, sitting hunched over at the counter, sipping at a cup of scalding coffee. The big man looked up and spotted Myra in the back mirror. He nodded his head imperceptibly; the woman hesitated for a moment, then joined McQ at the counter. The coffee shop stood in a mixed neighborhood, and a handful of black faces showed among the white ones having lunch.

"Got here as soon as I could, Lon," Myra apologized. "I had to stop by the bar."

"Want something to eat?"

"Coffee'll be fine."

McQ stood up and addressed the counterman. "Will you bring us some coffee, please?" He took his cup in one hand and Myra's arm in the other, and led her to a corner booth.

Squeezing into the booth, Myra remarked, "I don't know if it's healthy being seen with you. I hear you're getting a lot of people mad."

McQ just grinned his reply, then his face grew serious. "Myra, you read about the drug heist? The hit on the state narco officers?"

"Sure. It's been all over TV."

"Santiago pulled it. It has some angles I don't want to go into, but Santiago had no way of knowing the when and the where of the drug movement. Somebody in the state narco department or someplace tipped him. Know anything about it?"

Myra looked solemn, even a little thrilled. "No. I haven't heard a word."

"Nothing from those out-of-state hard rocks?"

"I doubt they knew. Why would Santiago tell them?" The counterman appeared, setting down a coffee cup for Myra and refilling McQ's cup from a Chemex.

"Thanks," said McQ, dismissing him. He turned his attention back to the woman.

"Myra, there's a rumor going around that somebody at headquarters isn't so clean. Somebody in a big chair."

Myra took a delicate sip at the too-hot coffee and backed away. "First I heard of it."

McQ looked dubious. "You wou'dn't be holding out on me, would you?" He remembered her methods of exacting payment. With a small, pleasant smile he added, "I'm a tired man."

Myra, catching his meaning, a'most blushed. But she looked at McQ sincerely. "No, I'm not dealing, Lon. But when you do get rested maybe you'll come by." The words were simple, but spoken in earnest and without provocation.

McQ looked over his coffee cup at the woman opposite and said softly, "You know something? You *are* pretty." And this time he wasn't lying.

Now Myra did blush. She was terribly pleased, but a realistic streak, strong in her personality, saved her from attributing too much to the compliment. Not that she didn't want to.

"Oh, sure. That's what a girl like me needs. A liar like you." She tossed her head at him flirtatiously. "I think I will have a hamburger, Lon. Might as well have him put some onions on it." It was her admission that she knew she'd be sleeping alone.

Rosey was at home. He must be, thought McQ, because his pimpmobile was parked at the curb outside his luxury apartment house, a customized Cadil'ac number with fancy scrollwork on its rose-pink body, and a fuschia vinyl roof over its gold-plated interior. Crime does not pay, mused McQ, and had to laugh.

He listened outside Rosey's apartment door, but heard nothing. All was quiet within. Taking out the handy little set of lock picks, he quietly and quickly let himself in and made his way through the apartment.

It was the apartment of a sensuous pig, no doubt about it. The dominant color was red; the walls covered in red velvet and the floors carpeted in two-inch-thick red velour. A huge sofa in the corner held a piled mass of red, pink and purple pillows, and red satin pillow-hassocks were strewn around for casual seating. Candles in twisted baroque holders stood everywhere; there were no overhead lights, but many lamps filtered their dim light through red silk shades. Dominating the room was a huge carved "home entertainment center," an eight-foot-long console that boasted a twenty-five-inch color TV and quadrophonic sound record player and tape deck. Smoky mirrors that had rivers of gold flowing through them covered three of the walls.

The bedroom was mirrored, too, on walls and ceilings, but here the glass was clear, not smoked, for maximum visibility. And here, in this pink palace of sex, a king-sized bed was the main and most appropriate piece of furniture. McQ, walking silently on the heavy carpeting, stood at the side of the bed, looking down at Rosey.

The black man lay naked on his back, sleeping soundly. On either side of him slept one of the foxes, also naked, cuddled up to Rosey's muscular body. McQ grinned, then he bent down and whipped the covers off. The girls woke on the instant, sitting up, startled, their youthful bodies gleaming black and pearly white in the bedroom gloom. Rosey was slower to wake up, and the girls shrieked and clutched at him.

McQ pushed the white girl out of the way and,

grabbing Rosey, dragged him to a sitting position. With both girls thrashing around and screaming at the tops of their healthy lungs, the action got a little muddled and McQ had the impression that there were eight or ten naked bodies tangling on the bed.

When she saw McQ clutching at Rosey, the black girl leaped at the tall detective, clawing for his eyes. "Let him go! Take your hands off him!"

He slapped her, hard, and turned to the other girl, ready to beat her, too. Both girls scrambled off the enormous bed and ran to the bathroom, locking themselves in.

Meanwhile, McQ turned back to Rosey, pouncing on him before he was fully awake. "Fornication," he shouted. "In double shots! *Sodomy!* Rosey, I think you're in trouble."

"Wha . . . ?" The black man was confused, his mind still drugged with sleep.

"Are you loaded?" demanded McQ. "Yeah, you're loaded, all right."

"What is this?" Rosey was coming awake. "You're no—"

"Let me hear you, Rosey. Let me hear how together you are. Say: 'I'm not a fig plucker or a fig plucker's son, but I'll pluck your figs until a fig plucker comes'." Shaking him by the shoulder like a rag doll, McQ urged, "Come on!"

Vulnerable in his nakedness and thoroughly confused, Rosey took a manful try at the tongue-twister. " 'I'm not a fig plucker or a fig plucker's son, but I'll pluck your figs until a fig plucker comes.' There!" he exclaimed, very pleased with himself for getting it right.

But McQ hurled him roughly against the head-board of the bed, demanding, "Faster!"

" 'I'm not a fig plucker or a fig plucker's son but I'll fuck your pigs until a pig fucker comes. . . !' "

"Obscene and offensive language," McQ ticked off in his most official voice. "Contributing to the delinquency of minors. . . ."

"*Minors!*?" howled Rosey, indignant as hell. "*Those* old bitches?"

Putting his battered face up close to the black man's, so that their noses almost touched, McQ hissed in his meanest tones, "Now listen to me, ass-hole. I hear your junk comes down to you from some brass at headquarters. Who?"

"What?" Rosey seemed genuinely puzzled.

"Come on, stupid, roll him over or you'll be squeaking soprano!" His big hairy hand made a threatening chop at the other man's exposed genitals.

"I don't know what you're talking about! I get from Santiago, you know that!"

"I think you do," snarled McQ. He squeezed the black man by the shoulder, twisting his steel-hard fin-gers into the tender muscles and nerves, seeing the hurt register on the other's face. "Let's hear it."

Rosey, his face contorted in pain, cried out, "Well, shit, man, if anybody was dirty you ought to know who . . . ."

McQ's fingers twisted more brutally. "What does that mean? Come on, spell it out."

"Boyle, that's who! Your partner! There's a dude who smelled bad all the way!"

McQ recoiled as the information registered. But he couldn't, wouldn't believe it without something more definite to go on. His fingers released Rosey's shoulder, but his voice took on an icy coldness that was terrible to hear. "What was that?"

Rosey, more frightened of the deadly tone than he had been of the heavy fingers, backed away on the bed. "Well, what I mean is—" he equivocated.

"Back it up for me. Come on, support it, Rosey, give me something hard."

But Rosey couldn't. "Talk," he mumbled. "That's all, just talk."

"Yeah," snarled McQ, "that's what I thought." He grabbed Rosey viciously, and shoved him up against the bedroom wall, putting his famous C-clamp hold on the black man's throat and tightening his fingers. "Try anything like that on me again, dummy, I'll squeeze your eyes out."

Tossing Rosey contemptuously back onto the bed, McQ turned to go. As he passed by the locked bathroom door, he called out, "You can come out now, ladies." He rapped on the door with his knuckles. "Go ahead, give him a nice disease."

Myra was sleeping alone, as she'd predicted, dead to the world, when the buzzer sounded. The insistent sound woke her eventually and she sat up, dazed. It buzzed again, louder and more insistent.

"Lon?" she yawned hopefully. "Just a minute, honey." She reached for her bathrobe and slipped it on. Stopping at the mirror, she took a quick and painful look at herself, making feeble attempts to fluff up her hair and dab on a spot of lipstick. Oh, how she wished she looked better! By now the buzzer was a steady, raucous peal.

"Just a second, I'm coming." she called out.

With something very close to joy, she opened the

door to Lon. But it wasn't Lon. It was an unrecognizable man, his features flattened and distorted by the stocking mask pulled over his head. Only the gun was recognizable, and it went off as Myra gasped, killing her instantly, and putting an end to her feeble vanity and even feebler hopes.

CHAPTER XIII

McQ kept the phone ringing long enough to satisfy himself that nobody was home. Then he stepped out of the phone booth and crossed the street to the large apartment building. He studied the line of doorbells, looking for the name and apartment number he wanted. There it was: Mr. and Mrs. E. Kosterman, Apt. 216.

It was the second to the left as you got out of the elevator into the beige-carpeted hallway. Using his set of lock picks, he had the door open in no time, and slipped inside. The Kostermans lived well, he noticed, as middle-class people without children usually do. The place was expensively decorated, but much too frilly for McQ's simple tastes. Too many pictures, too many knicknacks, everything exactly in its place—the whole apartment had a sterile look, like a picture in one of those magazines you buy in supermarkets.

Two Siamese cats came to the door to greet McQ, and the big man and the small animals regarded each other solemnly for a moment. Then McQ crossed the living room and pulled shut the drapes, closing the room in with darkness, so that neither he nor his flashlight could be seen from the street. McQ used a penlight, with a narrow but powerful beam, and he worked quickly, looking for evidence of some kind. Of what, he wasn't quite sure himself. He rummaged through Kosterman's desk, looking through letters, papers, bills and other minor documents, but finding nothing of any value. He turned his attention to other drawers, while the Siamese cats trotted at his heels, just as nosy as McQ.

Outside his apartment building, Ed Kosterman drove up and parked his car. Climbing out, he walked around the car and opened the door for his wife, a courteous gesture that she always enjoyed and even insisted upon. They had been to an official city dinner, and Helen was wearing a long dress and fur wrap; Kosterman himself looked trimmer than usual in his dinner jacket. As they headed for the house, the captain chanced to glance up, and noticed that the drapes in his apartment were closed. He checked both sets of windows. Drapes pulled shut. Odd, thought Kosterman, he didn't remember either of them pulling the drapes.

With a policeman's instinct, he turned to his wife. "Wait here, Helen." Obedient as always, she gave way without question, but looked after him with some concern as he crossed the street to their home.

Kosterman ignored the elevator and crept quietly up the stairs. Approaching his apartment, he drew out the gun he wore at all times, even with formal clothes. He turned the knob very slowly, feeling the door, which he'd left locked, yielding easily. Then he pushed open the door and with the same forward thrust of his shoulders hurled himself inside, gun at the ready. The Siamese cats uttered strident yells of fright and scattered. Except for the cats, the place was empty.

He stopped in the middle of the living room, feeling rather foolish. Then Kosterman noticed that the drapes were open again, and so was the window. He ran across the room and looked down at the street. It was empty too, in every direction. There was nobody in sight. Whoever had been there had jumped and vanished. And somebody had been there all right. All the drawers were open. But who would rob a police captain?

Pinky grabbed the phone on the first ring; he'd been sitting beside it all night, waiting for the call and smoking one cigarette after another.

"Pinky . . ." said McQ's voice.

"Lon, where the hell are you?" interrupted Farrow, his voice choked with distress. "I've been trying to reach you. What did Myra tell you?"

"Nothing. She didn't know a thing."

"Somebody thought she did," retorted Pinky. "She's been killed."

A click sounded in his ear. McQ had hung up.

Pinky's words had hit him hard. McQ leaned against the side of the phone booth, suddenly feeling very tired and low, almost like an old man. His spirits sank for the first time since Stan's death. Anger and bitterness flooded over him. Myra was dead and he himself was no further along.

He turned the Pontiac off the avenue and into the narrow street that led to his apartment building. Inside, McQ was still seething with frustration. Eveerything had turned up zilch tonight; nothing at Kosterman's, nothing from Rosey and now there would be nothing ever again—of any kind—from poor Myra. He pounded his fist on the wheel, remembering Rosey's nasty cracks about Stan. This night was a mother all around, and he'd be glad when it was over.

Halfway down the street, he pulled to a sudden stop. Up ahead, but still a fair distance away, a huge truck was coming from the other direction. But it was a one-way street, and the truck coming toward him was going the wrong way. And there'd be no room to pass. Irritated, McQ banged on the horn to alert the driver, but the heavy truck came on fast, lights blazing and engine roaring.

McQ caught on. It was coming for him, *at* him. Shoving the Pontiac into reverse, he started to back down the narrow street, glancing out the back window to make sure that nothing was coming .

But something was coming. A second truck, as large as the first, had turned off the avenue and was turning into McQ's street, only yards behind him. McQ hit the brake, hard. Suddenly he knew what this was all about. He was being sandwiched! Ahead of him, the first truck was still bearing down. Behind him, the second one was closing in fast. McQ hastily unbuckled his seat belt and opened the door of the death trap. But it was too late. The massive front of the heavy truck slammed into the front of the TransAm, the impact driving it backwards a few feet. Then the second truck plowed into McQ from behind, shaking the car and McQ, who was trapped inside.

The first truck, having backed off, went into forward gear again and smashed into the Pontiac a second time. Banged around inside like a jumping bean in a rattle and trapped with no hope of escape, McQ knew he had to do something fast. But what? He tried the door handle but it wouldn't work, jammed by the beating the car was taking. The second truck struck his rear again; and McQ's head slammed into the windshield for a nasty crack.

He reached out and turned on the burglar alarm system, then rolled his large body in the smallest, tightest ball possible and got down on the floor of the car. Back and forth the Pontiac shuddered as it was pounded this way and that by the attacking vehicles. The alarm sounded shrilly, as though the car were being beaten to death, which was exactly the case, while McQ's curled body was bashed again and again by the impacts.

Responding to the sound of the burglar alarm, a black and white patrol car turned into the narrow street, lights flashing and siren on full. At once the drivers of the heavy trucks leaped out of their cabs and ran like hell. The two officers, discovering that pursuit was hopeless, turned their attention to the battered, smashed mess that had once been McQ's pride and joy. They'd never seen anything like it before. Wait! Could something be moving in there?

Surely nobody could have survived? It didn't seem possible, but they'd better check.

It took hours and an oxyacetelyne torch to get McQ out. Workmen took turns, going slowly and carefully, while the ambulance and tow truck stood by. Three patrol cars kept the small crowd of gawkers in order. The narrow street had never been so crowded.

When the worker with the acetelyne torch had finished, somebody else moved in with a crowbar, and another half-hour passed before the can was opened and the single, badly battered sardine was extricated. The stretcher rolled up, and McQ found himself staring into J.C.'s dark, concerned face.

"I'm all right," he insisted. "I'm okay." But it was evident to J.C. and the ambulance attendants that McQ was dazed and hardly knew what he was saying. They loaded the big man into the ambulance, and J. C. went along for the ride. As the ambulance drove off, the young black man could see the tow truck craning up the remains of the Pontiac to haul it off.

It was not as bad as they'd feared. "How're you feeling?" the doctor asked. He was a young man, a recent medical-school graduate, and his long hair brushed the collar of his white smock. He smiled at McQ from around his handlebar moustache.

"Not bad," the big man drawled.

"Well, you're a lucky man. Nothing broken. No internal bleeding as far as we can tell. But cool it for a while. I want to look at you again later."

"Sure."

The young doctor turned to J.C., who sat perched

at the foot of McQ's bed. "Don't stay too long. Let him rest." He gave the nurse a few instructions in an undertone, and left.

"What's with the car?" McQ wanted to know.

J.C. shook his handsome head. "Total. You're going to need new wheels, that's for sure."

"Time I got rid of it anyway," McQ replied. "If it's not being wrecked, it's being stolen." A thought struck him suddenly, and he fell back on the pillow, his brow creased.

"What is it?" asked J.C. McQ just shook his head.

"If you want anything, Mr. McQ, you just ring," offered the nurse.

J. C. waited until she was out the door, then turned to McQ. "What do you think, Lon? Santiago?"

"Nope. He could have done me before if he wanted to."

"Well, the whole thing's bizarre. Why press you in iron?"

"Not so bizarre," said McQ. "Not if they wanted to separate me from the car. Where is it?"

"Impound garage on Olive. Why?"

"Just a thought." His head dropped back on the pillow.

J.C. waited for a minute, but it was obvious that nothing more would be forthcoming from McQ. He stood up. "Okay, I'll split. If you want anything, I'll be at home."

"Thanks, Jimmy." McQ managed a smile. "Say hello to Ellen."

After J.C. left, McQ spent a few minutes rapt in

thought. Then he reached for his bedside phone and dialed a number.

"Pinky, meet me at the impound garage on Olive as soon as you can. . . . Tell you then." He hung up and reached for his pants.

Getting out of the hospital was no major problem; he found the fire stairs easily and loped down them to the main floor, then ducked out the side door and hailed a taxi. As he drove off, he didn't bother to look back, so he didn't see the dark figure that stepped out of the shadows and looked long and hard after the taxi. It was J.C.

McQ got out at the corner; an old tracker's instinct insisted that he never take a taxi directly to his destination. After he paid off the driver, he stood and watched him drive away, then walked down the block and crossed the street to the garage. Pinky wasn't in sight, but McQ didn't wait. The garage was locked up for the night, but McQ made his way along the front of the building until he came to the small hut that sheltered the security guard.

The lights were on, and music was playing from a small table radio. But the hut was empty. Spread out on the table was an unwrapped sandwich, partially eaten, and an open thermos, steam still curling up from the hot liquid inside. A lunch box also stood on the table. Obviously, the guard's meal had been interrupted, and recently, from the look of it. But the room was very empty. McQ didn't like it.

He turned away from the security hut and inched along the chain-link fence that protected the parking area. No guard. No Pinky. Nobody. He took a short jump and clung to the fence, climbing over it without difficulty, and dropping down to the other side.

The parking area was jammed with cars—some smashed, some stolen, some towed away for parking violations. There were even a couple of police patrol cars parked there. Carefully, aware that the guard was around somewhere, McQ picked his way around the cars in the darkness, looking for what the trucks had left of his Pontiac TransAm. It took him a few minutes, but at last he found it, a smashed and hopeless pile of debris. It cost McQ a pang when he remembered how dashing and cavalier it had once been. Remembering his own bruises, he concluded that they'd both seen better days, and that neither one would ever be the same again.

He looked around once more for the officer who should be patrolling, but nobody was in sight. Turning his attention back to his car, McQ walked all around it, studying it from every angle, then climbed inside.

He ran his hand down inside the seats, then slashed at the vinyl with his pocket knife. Nothing. He ripped out the door panels. Nothing. The roof lining. Nothing. The back of the glove compartment. Nothing. He pulled up the carpeting and felt around the center hump that held the stick shift. Nothing. All this searching seemed to no avail; was it possible that nothing had been hidden in the car? McQ didn't think so.

Climbing out, he moved around the back of the car to the trunk. It was bent, and the lock wouldn't respond to McQ's key. Flexing his shoulders and exerting enormous strength, McQ ripped open the trunk with a great, tearing sound of protesting steel. Looking around quickly to see if the noise would bring the security guard, he froze in the darkness, waiting. Nobody came.

There seemed to be nothing unusual in the trunk, it was full of McQ's usual complement of debris and useful articles. Pushing the stuff aside, he pried up the section of the flooring that hid the secret compartment. The Mauser 7.63 still sat there, just as he'd left it. He lifted it out lovingly, and filled his pockets with ammo. But as he turned away from the trunk, something about it disturbed him, a wisp of memory he couldn't quite catch, something different that eluded him.

He had it now! Looking back into the trunk, he knew what was wrong. The spare tire was missing! What in the hell—? McQ turned away from the car and began to explore the area surrounding it, looking for the tire. Suddenly he tensed. There it was, on the floor! And beside the distinctive white-walled tire that matched the four on the Pontiac, a body! It was lying face down, the back of the head bashed in and bloody. Blood covered the shoulders and stained the back of the uniform, and McQ realized that sandwich would never get eaten now. Next to the body of the security guard lay a tire iron; it too was bloody.

There was nothing he could do for the man; the stillness of his body testified that he was beyond help. McQ knelt beside the tire, working his hand into the inside of it. Drawing out his fingers, he examined them. A white, powdery substance clung to them; McQ lifted it to his lips and licked it. No mistaking it: it was heroin.

He stood up like a shot. This was fantastic, a development he'd never considered in his wildest speculations! The dope had been in his car, and McQ himself had been driving it around!

Outside the impound garage, the streets had begun to fill up. Patrol cars glided in from all directions, flashers off and sirens silent. Quietly, officers climbed out of the cars and began to position themselves around the chain-link fence. Kosterman and J.C. got out of one car, Kosterman signaling for silence, and ordering his men to their stations by gesture only.

Yet even the most silent movement is still movement. McQ turned from contemplating the mysterious tire and his eye caught something flitting across the tail of it. He froze, and stood watching the policemen taking up their posts around the chain-link fence.

Suddenly, McQ realized the magnitude of the trouble he was in. There he stood, up to his asshole in dope that was stashed in a tire unmistakably his. Then, there was the matter of the dead body at his feet. Could it get any worse? Only if he'd also kidnapped Chief Grogan's five-year-old grandchild, and was found beating the kid. He moved off swiftly, looking for any possible route of escape.

Outside, Pinky Farrow had finally turned up. As he stepped out of his car, he looked around, puzzled, at the small army of police officers deployed around the garage. Before he could take another step, one of the officers stopped him.

"What's going on, officer?" asked the bewildered Pinky.

"Sorry, sir, you'll have to stay back," was the only reply.

Pinky spotted J.C. standing by Kosterman and yelled to him. "Jimmy. . . ."

The young black man turned at the sound of his name and walked over to Farrow.

"What is this?" Pinky demanded.

"Lon's in there," said J.C.

"I know. He phoned me to meet him here." He waved his hand at the crowd of police. "What's it all about?"

"You're not going to like this," J.C. said gravely. "We got an anonymous phone call saying Lon's been hauling a heavy load of dope in his car and he's come to get it."

Pinky shook his head in startled denial, speechless.

By now, everything was ready. "Okay! Throw on the lights!" yelled Kosterman, reaching for his bullhorn. At once the spotlights mounted on the top of every deployed police vehicle snapped on, turning their full battery of power on the impound garage.

As the lights flashed on, McQ dropped down, instinctively, seeking the cover of the automobiles In a crouch, he moved forward a few feet, then stopped, stymied. Up ahead was the link fence and right in front of it, policemen at the ready.

"Lon . . . we know you're in there." Kosterman's voice filled the garage, amplified many times by the bullhorn. "Come out and there won't be any trouble."

No trouble for *you*, McQ thought. But for McQ? With a dead security guard and a load of heroin? There would be trouble all right, and plenty of it. He ran quickly in another direction, still crouching low. More police. Shit.

"Okay," yelled Kosterman. "Unlock the gate and sweep it!" One officer ran forward and unlocked the gate, swinging it wide. Others ran through it into the parking area, spreading out for the sweeping search. Kosterman remained stationed at his car, awaiting results, not saying a word to J.C. or Pinky. The three formed an anxious, silent group.

The police swept forward, searching through and around the cars, even under them. Crouched behind the wheel of one of the police patrol cars in the garage, McQ desperately manipulated wires, trying to ignite the spark that jumped the engine. Through the windshield he could see the sweep coming closer and closer.

By now they had found the body of the security guard. "Better call the captain." The officer drew his gun; now he knew that McQ would stop at nothing. The search intensified; every officer prepared to shoot on sight.

Suddenly the patrol-car engine roared into life and the vehicle leaped forward out of its parking space. With McQ driving hell-for-leather, it headed at top speed toward the open gate.

McQ came barreling through the gate, right by J.C., Pinky and Kosterman, whose jaw dropped in disbelief as he saw the face of the driver speeding past. "Christ!" shrieked Kosterman. "There he goes in a black and white!" Police officers came charging out of the parking lot after him, firing. The men in the patrol cars ringed around the garage began firing too, at close range as McQ headed for them.

Zigzagging like a broken field runner, McQ rushed headlong at the patrol cars, side-swiping first one and then another, and sending them spinning around crazily. Some officers ran for their cars to give chase, while Kosterman grabbed up his police-car radio to call in his instructions. The scene was bedlam; car engines, shouting men, the futile ring of wasted bullets.

McQ rounded the corner on two wheels, tires screeching, and headed up the steep hill ahead of him. Behind him, he could hear the chase beginning as police car after police car pulled out after him. When he reached the crest, McQ slowed down just enough to get out of the patrol car, on the run. Carrying the Mauser, he sprinted for the cover of a nearby building. The driverless police car kept on going, over the crest and down the hill on the other side, crashing headlong through the wooden walls of a warehouse and disappearing out of sight inside.

Cresting the hill, the police officers saw their quarry crash and raced down to the warehouse after McQ, fanning out to search the building. From the safety of his hiding place above them on the hill, McQ watched in silence until he was certain that nobody else was following. Then he took off, the Mauser tucked under his arm.

CHAPTER XIV

The janitor helped Lois carry out her luggage; she managed her purse and a small suitcase easily, while he puffed along with the three large heavy bags. They stopped in front of Lois's red Plymouth parked toward the front of her apartment-house garage.

"Back seat'll be fine," said Lois.

"Yes, ma'am." He stowed them all neatly inside, and held out his hand for the two dollars that Lois had ready.

"Thank you, George."

"Thank you, Mrs. Boyle. Have a nice trip." He disappeared to buy himself a drink.

Lois walked around the car to the driver's side, stopping, startled, one hand on the door handle. Standing in the back of the garage was McQ, holding a large automatic pistol. His clothes were a mess and his face sported a whole new set of welts and bruises. All in all, he looked like he'd just done six rounds with a killer shark. It must have been some fight.

"Lon!" she exclaimed, a worried look on her face.

"Where are you going?" he asked her.

"Down to see my folks."

"Okay. Back the car in and open the trunk."

"What happened?"

"Lois, come on," he urged. It was no time for explanations.

Realizing this, Lois nodded and got into the car, backing it up to where McQ stood. Leaving the trunk open, he climbed in, and, with his pocket knife, cut a generous air hole in the plastic partition between the trunk and the rear interior of Lois's car.

"Okay," he said as he finished cutting. "Shut the trunk and let's go."

The red Plymouth moved along smoothly, heading south. Lois drove as steadily as she could, avoiding sudden starts and stops, never swerving, and keeping her eye open for bumps and potholes. Nevertheless, McQ was hardly comfortable. Six feet five inches of man is a helluva lot to squeeze into even the most commodious trunk, and every muscle in his body was cramped and protesting with twinges. Also, he was slightly sick at his stomach from the rolling.

Up ahead was the toll gate. Through the windshield, Lois could see a couple of patrol cars; police officers were checking every car that passed through the toll point.

"Lon, there're some officers at the toll gate."

"You're okay," replied the muffled voice. "You're on a trip."

Lois drew up to the line of cars and took her place. As she waited, she betrayed her nervousness by drumming impatiently on the steering wheel, but when her turn came, she pulled herself together. Stopping at the booth, she paid her toll with an air of unconcern, even smiling at the policeman who poked his head into the car to check her out.

"Thank you, ma'am," he said, returning the smile.

She pulled out of the booth and onto the bridge, crossing it without incident and making for the freeway. After they had gone some sixty miles south and the road was clear, Lois pulled onto a shoulder and opened the trunk. A very rumpled McQ, sore in every limb, got out and stretched, then climbed into the passenger seat, breathing deeply to fill his aching lungs with air.

"All right, what happened?" asked Lois.

McQ didn't answer. He'd pieced a lot of it together by now, not all, but a lot, and many of the answers weighed heavily on him, causing him pain.

"Lon, for God's sake . . ." Lois urged.

"Stan was dirty."

Shocked, she turned her eyes away from the road ahead of her and onto McQ's face. It bore the marks of the struggle going on inside him, and she kept her mouth shut and let him continue.

"A snitch told me; I didn't believe it. I bled him pretty good for saying it. . . ."

"I don't believe it," Lois stated firmly.

"He was on a frolic to switch dope out of the property section and sell it off."

"No, it's a mistake! Stan was an honest cop." Lois's voice held a pleading note.

"What dishonest cop wasn't, once upon a time?

Lois, the dope had been stashed in my spare tire. I'd been hauling it around for days."

But Lois still protested. "What did Stan have to do with that?"

"Everything. I'd loaned him my car. He said his was in the shop. That's how the junk got there. Of course, I'd never known if he hadn't been killed. He'd simply have moved it on."

"You really mean it, don't you?" she asked, wonder mingling with the hurt in her voice.

"All the way. Feel pretty silly, too. All that time playing the avenging angel."

There was a moment of silence in the car, then Lois sighed. "Well, I suppose it was my fault. Partly, anyway. Complaining about the life, the pay. I guess he thought a big crop would have brought me back to him. . . . I'm glad he's dead." Then her voice grew firmer. "But I tell you this. I'm on his side." A strong note of bitterness crept into her words. "Why not? It's the new national sport. Called 'grabbing.' Whatever happened to baseball? Everybody plays it. All you need is position and a good one is 'public trust.' So the senator sells privileges and the judge takes bribes and that Southern governor spends public funds for banquet dinners." She laughed, marveling at the insanity of it. "Banquet dinners! The only puzzlement there is that he doesn't end up in the Cabinet. So what do you expect? Some place along the line your local librarian is going to fall . . . and the cop. In this case it happened to be Stan."

"And some others," drawled McQ.

"Who?"

"Somebody tall, somebody in. Somebody who had Wally Johnson and Stan killed to have more for himself. Who had beat officer Hyatt taken off to make the murders look random and throw it on militants."

"Kosterman?" asked Lois, her eyes on the road.

"That's what I'll find out."

"How?"

McQ didn't answer right away. This information hurt, too, turning his insides around and making him come up empty.

"Through you," he said.

Lois looked sharply at him, trying to read the expression on his face.

"I feel pretty silly about that, too," he said.

"Lon, you're crazy . . ." Lois began.

"That would be nice," McQ interrupted. "I'd like that better. No, it started to play back to me. How you kept saying 'let's get in your car and go someplace.' My car. Not once, twice at least. You were in it together but Stan got double-dealt. You not only took him off your belly, you took him out of this world. You and your new 'partner'—"

Lois interrupted his accusation, "You *are* crazy."

"Well, we'll see. I'll just stick with you, Lois, and see who shows up to get the junk." He flashed her a small, cold, tight smile devoid of mirth. Then, reaching around into the back seat, he picked up one of the suitcases. "Which one's it in? This one?"

McQ tried to open the suitcase, but it was locked. He looked at Lois, but she refused to return his glance, sitting tight-lipped at the wheel, her eyes fixed on the road. With a shrug, McQ rolled down the window on his side and poised the suitcase on the window edge. He checked Lois's reaction again; there wasn't any. He gave the case a push and it tumbled out of the window onto the highway, breaking open.

Clothes spilled out, their bright colors making a rainbow splash on the road.

Glancing at Lois, McQ reached back and picked up suitcase number two. It, too, was locked. Lois kept her eyes firmly ahead of her, refusing to so much as look at him. Her hands clenched the steering wheel so tightly that her knuckles showed white under the skin. McQ hurled the second bag out of the car window; it bounced along the highway for a few feet, then broke open, spilling out its contents. More women's clothing.

McQ looked steadily at Lois, but she showed no reaction at the destruction of her wardrobe. Any other woman would be yelling her head off. He reached for the third suitcase.

The black sedan sat parked several blocks away from the highway, just near enough to see the cars that passed. A minute after Lois went by, its engine coughed into life and it moved forward smoothly, turning onto the highway after her. It was in no hurry; its destination was secure, so why rush? Following Lois, the sedan let a good distance open up between them, but kept the red Plymouth in sight.

McQ held the third suitcase poised at the edge of the open window, ready to push.

"Lon, for God's sake, there's two million dollars there!" Lois's voice was sharp, almost hysterical.

He stopped the push and, steadying the bag, pulled it back in. He was right. This was the suitcase with the junk.

"Lon," Lois wheedled in a tone of reason, "you like me. I like you. I don't have to see my folks. I can go anyplace. We can go together." As she spoke, her eyes unconsciously sought the rear-view mirror, a tiny action that McQ did not fail to notice. He turned and looked through the back window of the car. Behind them, as far back as possible yet still in sight, the black sedan was merely a speck. McQ could not make out the driver, nor could the driver of the sedan see that somebody was in the car with Lois.

"Speed up," McQ ordered.

With one quick glance at McQ, Lois picked up speed. McQ crouched low beside her in the seat so that he wouldn't be seen by the shadowing car. He had no idea whose car it was, nor did he know that from its window had come the shotgun blast that had killed Stan Boyle.

McQ looked out the side window, checking the terrain. They were traveling along the side of a huge salt company's solar-evaporation plant, 50,000 acres of tidal marshland used for the production of salt. The country was vast, flat, open, a series of shallow saltwater ponds and levees, traversed by miles of dike roads. By means of the levees, saltwater from the sea was circulated through the shallow ponds for evaporation, crystalization and eventual harvesting and processing.

The marshes were also a wildlife sanctuary, where thousands of ducks, rails, marsh hawks, gulls and bitterns fed on the fish and shellfish of the ponds. The flat marshlands were covered with stiff, hardy grasses —alkali bulrush, glasswort and arrow grass—and teeming with small animal, bird and insect life. Every year, birds came down the Pacific flyway in tens of thousands to nest and breed in these wetlands.

McQ glanced out of the rear window. The sedan,

too, had speeded up, and was cutting down the distance between the two cars.

"Turn off onto the work road," McQ ordered. Lois obeyed, and the Plymouth began to cross the dikes that criss-crossed the salt ponds. McQ observed the sedan still tailing, turning off the highway onto the work road, too.

McQ faced front, checking his Mauser to be sure it was loaded and ready. He smiled a little, with satisfaction. He was in good shape. He had the dope, he had the monster gun, and now he was going to get Lois's partner. That would just about wrap things up.

"Okay, now stop the car," he ordered. Lois shot him an angry glance and kept on driving. With one deft motion, McQ reached over her, switched off the ignition and pocketed the key. The Plymouth slowed down, and rolled gradually to a stop. Mauser ready, McQ crouched down so the driver of the black sedan wouldn't see him as the car came closer. He could see now that there was only one man in the car, but he couldn't yet make out whom.

The black sedan pulled up alongside Lois's car. "McQ! He's in the car!" Lois yelled a warning out the window.

The driver of the sedan leaned down hard on the accelerator and dug out backwards, starting away from Lois's Plymouth. McQ bounded out, clutching the Mauser, and opened fire on the receding sedan. His shots blew out one of the black car's rear tires, and the vehicle went out of control, swerving and skidding across the narrow road and coming to a stop at right angles to the roadway. The driver scrambled out and, before McQ could get a good look at him, dashed behind his car, using it as a cover, and opening fire on McQ.

As the bullets whizzed around them, Lois ducked down on the front seat, seeking protection, while McQ used the Plymouth as a shield, watching the bullets thunk into it. Now he held his fire, thinking. It appeared to be a stalemate, with both gunmen hiding behind their cars. McQ was determined to break it, but he wasn't anxious to get killed.

Suddenly making up his mind, McQ threw himself down on his belly, peering under the Plymouth at the sedan. All he could see was the driver's legs and feet, but that was all he'd expected and all he was going to need. Taking careful aim with the Mauser, he pressed the trigger of the automatic pistol and fired.

His shots destroyed the unseen man's ankles and shins. Screaming with pain, he sank to the ground, making a valiant effort to bring his gun around and fire. But now his entire body was in McQ's sights, and he let him have it. The Mauser chattered and the body went limp. The man was dead.

McQ rose from the ground and began to reload his Mauser. He turned as Lois got out of the car and looked at him bleakly. Then she ran toward the black sedan and around behind it, where the body lay. His gun ready again, McQ followed her slowly. He walked around the car and took a look at the man he had just killed. Lois stood shaken, staring down at the crumpled figure who lay with his face in the dirt. McQ put his foot out and turned the man over.

It was a tall man all right, but it wasn't Kosterman. As a matter of fact, it wasn't even a police officer.

The dead man was Franklin Toms, liaison officer to the mayor. His once-elegant figure was now torn and dirty and covered with blood. He would have loathed himself if he could have seen himself.

"Yeah," McQ said softly, "Servant of the People."

He looked at Lois Boyle. Her eyes were misted over with tears, her slim body limp. She seemed drained of everything, all the spirit and fire gone out of her. McQ suddenly realized that there was more to her relationship with Toms than merely the caper. Although she appeared hardly capable of listening, McQ ticked off the end of the story for Lois.

"He killed Myra figuring maybe she knew about it from Stan. He took off the impound-garage guard to get the dope, tipped the police I was there, turned the junk over to you for safe transport out, planning to meet you later. Too bad. You get to go the rest of the way alone."

Lois looked at McQ, her face a dead mask empty of emotion. Taking her firmly by the arm, he led her to the car and shoved her into the passenger seat, getting behind the wheel himself. He bent to turn the key in the ignition and started up the car. When he looked up, McQ spotted something in the rearview mirror. A speck, but getting larger every second. Coming up fast, barreling along the work road, coming closer and closer. It was Santiago's Mercedes.

CHAPTER XV

Santiago! McQ didn't like this; he had this case all wrapped up pretty, just as he'd figured. Now this was one complication too many, one that he hadn't counted on. He shoved the Plymouth into gear and stepped on the gas. But Tom's sedan was blocking the way and Santiago's Mercedes was coming up faster than ever.

Gritting his teeth, McQ floored the gas pedal and plowed headlong into the sedan, hitting it hard from the rear and literally shoving it off the road. The sedan nosed forward off the narrow dike road and plowed into an evaporating pond, where it sank a few feet and sat, half submerged, like a frog under a lily pad.

Behind him, McQ could just make out that there

were five men in the pursuing Mercedes, Santiago and four of his hoods. He pushed for as much speed as he could get out of Lois's car, even though its engine was no match for the powerful German car behind them. Although they were still some distance apart, Santiago was quickly closing that distance.

The dike roads were extremely narrow, and highly dangerous at fast speeds. On either side were the salt ponds and, as the Plymouth rushed past them, ducks rose into the air squawking with terror, their iridescent wings make a rushing, beating sound.

Now, Santiago was closing ground with every second; McQ, trying desperately, wasn't able to coax any more speed or power out of the Plymouth than he was already getting. He was worried, but he kept his eyes fixed on the narrow, winding and hazardous road in front of him. Lois, turning back anxiously to look at the Mercedes, let out a gasp of fear. McQ, checking in his rear-view mirror, saw that the car was much closer, and that the nasty gleam of a shotgun barrel was coming from the Mercedes' window.

Taking careful aim despite the bouncing of the Mercedes, the shotgun man squeezed the trigger and fired. The blast hit the Plymouth solidly in the gas tank, causing an explosion and immediate fire. The car went out of McQ's control; it swerved wildly off the dike road and nosed into the pond, sinking in about a foot, still burning.

Grabbing the Mauser and the suitcase with the dope, McQ burst from the Plymouth, hollering "Come on!" at Lois. Her face white with terror, the girl scrambled after him out of the burning vehicle. Ankle-deep in the salt pond, splashing salt and water with every step, the pair ran as fast as they could across the pond to the far end. They were hampered by the sluggish water pulling at their feet, but ahead of them they could see solid ground and the salt-processing plant.

The Mercedes came to a sliding, screeching halt near Lois's burning Plymouth. Santiago and his four hoods jumped out, their guns drawn, taking aim on their awkwardly moving targets.

Bullets spattered around McQ and Lois as they sloshed through the thick, evaporating water encrusted with salt. Shoving Lois down into the salt, McQ flopped down himself, whirling to open fire with his Mauser automatic pistol.

Santiago and his men were now pursuing their quarry through the pond, and the sudden rain of bullets from McQ caught them unaware. One of the hoods, hit, fell forward with a choked cry, landing on his face in the salt, where he lay still. Santiago and the others dropped low, crouching into the pond for cover.

At the far end, Lois and McQ scrambled out of the pond and up its steep bank. Ahead of them was the plant and its machinery and near it an immense salt mound. Washed from the water, the crude salt was as white as snow and formed a mountain about twenty feet high, composed of almost three hundred thousand pounds of tidal salt. Pushing Lois ahead of him, McQ yelled for her to keep moving. Still lugging the heavy dope suitcase and clutching his Mauser, McQ made for the salt mound; he and Lois threw themselves behind it for cover.

Their footing heavy, Santiago and his three remaining men sloshed across the pond, keeping low. As they reached the far edge and began to scramble out, a chatter of gunfire from McQ's Mauser pinned them down, and they ducked behind the pond's steep bank, protected by the high rise of its perimeter.

McQ broke open the Mauser and reloaded it with the ammo clip from his pocket. He could hear Santiago calling to him from his crouched cover in the pond.

"McQ, can you hear me? I want the suitcase."

Making no reply, the tall man finished reloading his powerful weapon. Santiago shouted again.

"Now come. Give it to me and there will be no trouble."

McQ glanced at Lois, but made no answer. The girl's eyes were filled with a mute appeal.

"I will *purchase* it from you," offered Santiago. "I will make you a business deal. Twenty-five cents on the dollar."

Behind the salt mound, Lois and McQ exchanged glances. Hers was begging openly. She still saw some hope of salvaging something. Knowing what she was thinking, McQ gave her no sign of what was going on in his head.

"Not satisfactory?" called Santiago. *"Fifty* cents on the dollar. Now that certainly is fair. You have the goods, I have the means of distribution. Come now, let us shake hands on the arrangement."

Santiago's voice ceased, and a heavy silence fell, a silence in which McQ was making up his mind. Ignoring the tremblings of anticipation on Lois's face, the tall detective suddenly stood up and stepped from behind the mound, a move so sudden it took Santiago's hoods by surprise. With all the might of his powerful muscles and masculine bulk, McQ raised the suitcase high and flung it toward Santiago.

"You want the damn thing? Okay, go and get it!" he hollered.

Lois, aghast, uttered a little moan as the case sailed through the air and landed in the pond a short distance from Santiago and his men. It sank a few inches under its weight and rested there. McQ ducked quickly behind the salt mound and watched.

Startled into indecision, Santiago just looked at the case, so near and yet so far. Lois, bewildered, wondered what McQ could hope to gain from this move. And McQ, silent as usual, just watched and waited. A long minute passed.

Then, in Spanish, Santiago commanded one of his men to get the case. Nervously wetting his lips and glancing around him, the hood started out as ordered. Crouched low, protected by the rise of higher land along the edge of the pond, the gunman sloshed cautiously through the pond to fetch back two million dollars worth of narcotics. It was slow going, and the hood took care to keep his body as low as possible, out of range of McQ's Mauser. Every few steps, he glanced back at the salt mound, but there was no sign of McQ. Once or twice he glanced back at Santiago, who merely gestured at him to continue.

Santiago's man came closer and closer to the suitcase, making his way through the heavy silence broken only by the slosh of the water sucking at his feet. At last he reached it and, with a last glance around him, grabbed it by the handle. Still crouching low, he started back with the drugs to Santiago.

The Mauser opened fire, the bullets ripping the suitcase open and spilling a trail of heroin. The terrified thug looked up; McQ was crouched *on top* of the twenty-foot mound, from which vantage point he had the perfect angle down to draw a bead. While the hood had been sloshing toward the suitcase, McQ had silently climbed the monumental tower of salt.

"There! There! Up there!" screamed the hood, pointing to McQ. A second burst of bullets from the Mauser found their target and the man pitched forward into the pond, dead. The suitcase tumbled into the water, where the salt, the water and the dope began to mingle.

Santiago's face turned livid; millions had been just within his grasp and now he saw them slipping away. Strangling on his words with rage, he lapsed into Spanish and snarled "Get him! Get him!"

He urged his two men up the bank and followed them, the three of them spreading out to attack McQ, using every available bit of cover, including tall clumps of marsh grass and processing machinery. McQ stood up to fire, ignoring the fact that he was more exposed. With a deadly accuracy, the Mauser found another target, and Santiago's third man, running, was stopped in his tracks and killed.

McQ fired another long burst, but Santiago had dived behind a tussock. The Mauser clicked. And again. The clip was empty. McQ stood on the top of the salt mound with two armed men still alive and a useless automatic weapon in his hands.

Sensing his advantage, Santiago urged his last remaining gunman: "Now! Now! Quick!"

Both men rushed forward from cover, each taking a different side of the mound. They scrambled forward in their eagerness to attack the tall man, who, vulnerable at last, stood with his empty Mauser dangling from one hand.

Lightning fast, McQ reached into his belt and

171

pulled out the snub-nosed .38 which, with the Mauser, he had "borrowed" from the police property section. With almost a single graceful movement, he fired twice at Santiago, then turned to fire two more times at the last gunman. The gun barked loudly, then silence fell.

McQ relaxed on the top of the mound, listening to the tentative sounds of the marsh birds. Below him, Manuel Santiago lay dead, sprawled on his back in a pile of salt. On the other side of the mound, the last gunman's body was also twisted in the unnatural posture of death.

The tall man skidded down the white mountain, salt scudding out like spray under his shoes. Lois Boyle stood looking with wide, terrified blue eyes at the corpse of Santiago and McQ took her by the arm. His touch wasn't brutal, but it wasn't gentle, either. He led her to the edge of the pond, where they could look down at the bullet-torn body of the man who'd gone for the suitcase. Next to him bobbed the ripped remains of the case, perforated with bullet holes. Salt water had leaked in and the dope had leaked out and mingled with both was the dead man's blood.

"You still want the junk?" McQ asked Lois. "Go ahead. Maybe you can get it with a strainer." Lois stared down at the body in shock, unable to reply.

They waited for him at the parking area behind headquarters, J.C., Pinky Farrow and Kosterman. When McQ got out of the police car, they pressed forward. Lon shook hands with Pinky and J.C., but Kosterman and he just exchanged long meaningful glances. The captain broke the silence.

"Okay, I had it wrong," he said crisply. He was too tough a man to be embarrassed.

"Something else, Lon," J.C. said with some hesitancy. It was very obvious that he *was* embarrassed. "I've been a loan-out to Internal Affairs. You were the subject. I was on you all along."

"I see," said McQ. He saw.

"No hard feelings?" the young black detective asked anxiously.

McQ shrugged his massive shoulders indecisively, but something in his face told J.C. that it wasn't hard feelings. Now Kosterman, the politico in action, slapped McQ on the shoulder, glossing over the whole affair.

"Oh, come on, it's all over . . . Lon, I want to see you get your shield back. Full reinstatement, back pay. . . ." He glanced up at McQ, who was not jumping at the offer. "Lon," Kosterman continued, "it's where you belong. Look, what else have you got?"

Even Kosterman, whose gall was immense, realized that saying McQ was empty was hardly the most tactful remark, and he lapsed into silence, the political smile still glued to his face.

"I'll think about it," said McQ.

Kosterman's smile faded, and he took his arm off McQ's shoulder. His own words had just been flung back in his teeth and he knew it. He stood bitterly watching the tall man as McQ and Pinky moved off together to Farrow's car.

"What's to think about?" Pinky wanted to know.

McQ drew a deep breath. "Well, look at it this way. There's still somebody in the state narco department who tipped Santiago on the drug movement."

"Yeah . . . " conceded Pinky.

"And Toms was too small to have laid it all out. Levels, Pinky. There's somebody sitting dirty in the Tower who gives the orders."   ,

This was a long speech for McQ, and he fell silent, watching Pinky struggle with the information, and with the enormity of the task that McQ was evidently assuming. The two men's eyes met; Pinky's glance held mingled admiration and apprehension.

"I think I'll just keep that space in your office. Okay?" asked McQ.

Pinky nodded, and they climbed into the older man's car. As they drove past City Hall Tower and the government buildings, Pinky saw a smile, starting small, widening until it was a grin, on McQ's, battered face. McQ was getting ready to roll.

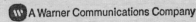